WHO WATCHES THE WATCHMEN?

Bridget R. Edwards

Rollo Books

Copyright © 2024 Bridget R. Edwards

All rights reserved

The characters and events portrayed in this book are fictitious. Any similarity to real persons, living or dead, is coincidental and not intended by the author.

No part of this book may be reproduced, or stored in a retrieval system, or transmitted in any form or by any means, electronic, mechanical, photocopying, recording, or otherwise, without express written permission of the publisher.

ISBN-13: 9798329727302

Cover design by: B.R. Pinto
Library of Congress Control Number: 2018675309
Printed in the United States of America

For James and Tim
(Who are TOTALLY AND COMPLETELY NOT like Peter and Caleb)

MARCH 2020

AAAAAARRRRRRRRRRRRRGGGGGGHHHHH!!!!!

I am sooooooooooooooooooooooooooo FURIOUS!!!!!

It is TOTALLY not fair! Why does everyone, I mean EVERYONE on this whole STINKING PLANET, blame me for EVERYTHING!

(Except for you, Razzy-Razzy-Rascal, you gorgeous FURBALL OF A CAT, you are the ONLY life form in the known universe who doesn't think that it's MY FAULT that everything's going wrong at the moment.)

To prove it, I'm going to make a list of "THINGS THAT CALEB TIMOTHY ASHBY IS BEING BLAMED FOR WHEN IT IS NOT HIS FAULT":

1) Climate change

This is my fault for just being BORN - according to Pete.

2) Seeing a ghost at After School Club

Now – not my fault at all!

It is ABSOLUTELY AND DEFINITELY TRUE (whatever Mrs Watkins says to Mum) that I saw the dinner lady ghost last Tuesday afternoon when I was at Afterschool Club. I saw her as clearly as I can see your ULTRA-FLUFFY head just now - she was standing there by the door to the GIRLS' TOILETS in her pink-checked jacket-thingy. Actually it wasn't very pink, more of a pinky-grey colour. Ooooo, hey, listen to this: it was the *ghost* of the COLOUR PINK!!!

And she was see-through – I mean, if you looked carefully you could see right through her body to the posters stuck on the wall behind her, which was, admittedly, PROPER WEIRD. But then she smiled and I felt okay about her and she told me she was called Vera.

And then she VANISHED – not like you do when you see Granny's dog with a quick whoosh and a flash of ginger fur but, like just PROPERLY gone in front of my eyes as I blinked.

But you need to realise that, in her FREAKY GHOSTY way, I knew she was kind and not a bit bad. And THAT'S what I told the Receptions at dinner time when they came down to the loos to wash their hands. I DEFINITELY wasn't trying to scare them – Mrs Watkins TOTALLY got it wrong.

(But then she's ALWAYS like that – she NEVER LISTENS when you're trying to explain something to her and she's always telling us that we NEVER LISTEN to her so she's ABSOLUTELY AND TOTALLY a hypocrite!!! And I have absolutely no idea how she ever got to be a head teacher cos she's just about THE DUMBEST person I have ever met in my whole life - except for Pete of course who's the biggest A-STAR MORON THICKO!!!!)

3) *You being sick just now.*

Pete reckons that it was COMPLETELY my fault you ate that dead pigeon and that I should have stopped you but as he is a super moron (see above) he fails to realise that it's your CAT-RIGHT to eat pigeons – dead or alive. And if you do eat them and puke up afterwards then you'll learn from the experience and WON'T DO IT AGAIN. Which is just what Dad is always saying to me when I do something like that - not eating dead pigeons OBVIOUSLY because that's disgusting (unless you actually are a cat).

4) *Peter being a moron*

Not my fault. Period.

5) *Storm Caleb, which is currently trying to blow our roof off.*

Just because the latest storm's got my name, it's NOTHING WHATSOEVER TO DO WITH ME. I mean, do I look like Thor the god of thunder? Actually it would be rather cool to be Thor but I'm not. I don't have a beard or a hammer - well I did have a hammer but then Dad said I had to put it back.

6) *This corona-virus thingy*

I bet you they'll blame me for this as well even though it's ONLY JUST BEEN DISCOVERED in a town called Wuhan which is in China or somewhere. No doubt Mrs Watkins will tell Mum that I flew over there and SNEEZED over someone, so all the Chinese people caught it, and so OF COURSE it's all my fault!

Actually Razzy, it is a bit freaky - they thought it might just stay in China like a good little virus, but then ha, it's escaped and has ended up all over the world so that the grown-ups are completely freaking about it cos IT'S GOT NO CURE!! (I've put some more exclamation marks in cos it really is kind of scary.)

There's these cruise ships where everyone on board has fallen ill and they've not been allowed to dock anywhere which is serious cos they are running out of water and food and duty-free Toblerones. And then in China, and now in Italy, there's all these people who've fallen properly sick. And so every night on the news you've got the Prime Minister with this 'I am so worried' look on his face, saying that loads more people are getting ill, and the hospitals are saying 'we haven't got enough beds to look after everybody who catches it'.

And they've cancelled the Eurovision Song Contest, I mean, how serious is that?

And in Ireland they have just CLOSED ALL THE SCHOOLS (lucky lucky Irish children). And they can't go out except for going to get food or medicine or for exercise (boo).

And they reckon that might happen here too...

(Please please please...!)

CHAPTER 1

It had been a crap evening.

In fact, Peter reckoned it might be classed as a totally crappy evening or an uber-crappy evening and might even turn out to be the uber-crappiest evening in the nearly-fourteen years of his existence.

It had started badly after school. He'd had another run-in with Jake Webb, a nasty piece of work who seemed to delight in picking on him. On Peter's way home from school, while he was passing the chippy, Webb and his precious little mates had snatched his bag and had thrown it over the canal bridge. Fortunately, it had landed on the deck of a moored narrowboat rather than in the water, but this had led to him having to sneak on board the boat to retrieve it, getting an earful from the dreadlocked bargee.

On arriving home, Rascal, their headstrong ginger cat, had brought a dead pigeon into the kitchen, eaten it and then thrown up all over the floor. Caleb, his nine-year-old brother, had refused to clear it up - saying that he would only be sick himself and had rushed off to hide when Peter threatened to punch him. So, Peter had ended up cleaning the floor, which made *him* want to puke.

Mum and Dad had come home thoroughly disgruntled. They had been summoned to Caleb's primary school because he had been telling the Receptions that their toilets were haunted. Caleb was insisting it was true and that he had actually seen the spook - the ghost of a long-dead dinner lady. But the Head was having none of it, especially as Caleb was already on a warning having been thrown out of Assembly the previous week for burping the hymns.

Mad as only Mum could be after a run-in with a teacher, she

had sent Caleb to his room and he was now bewailing his lot to the cat, claiming to be a neglected child.

And then there was Mum's news.

By nine pm the long-forecasted (and aptly named) Storm Caleb was raging round their house. But despite the wind wailing like a demented banshee down the dale outside, it was a mere breeze to the hurricane-force row his parents were having downstairs in the kitchen.

Looking out from his bedroom window over the dark garden, he could hear the sinister creaking of the trees. He swore loudly at the ferocious night, savouring the sound of the expletive, feeling that if you were nearly fourteen, it was right to swear on such a night as this. The word was echoed immediately – his brother had come into the room, his dark brown fringe quiffed up like the tail of a frightened cat.

"Get lost, Cay. And you're not supposed to swear."

"I can if you can. Anyway - it's not like *they're* not swearing!"

They listened to the colourful language coming up the stairs. Peter had to admit that Caleb had a point. He moved up to let him see out of the window.

"Why did you have to wind the little 'uns up about that ghost? That's what's put Mum and Dad in such a bad mood."

"But there is a ghost! She's called Vera and for some reason she haunts the bogs when everyone's gone home, and I'm investigating why."

"How can you investigate something that doesn't exist. You are a complete weirdo. And stop shoving me out of the way!"

"Vera does exist! And you're completely totally blocking the window, you arch-moron!"

"Am not, arch-moron yourself!"

Their fight was punctuated by another blast of argument from downstairs. It was their mother's voice, sounding shrill as she warmed to her theme.

"The reason I didn't tell you I was going for the job is precisely this! You'd have thrown a hissy fit and I wouldn't have even put in the application. At least now I've been offered the job, we have a choice."

The door to the kitchen slammed and the voices faded.

Caleb looked up at his brother scared. His face was pale in the flickering moonlight and dotted with freckles. "They're not going to get divorced, are they?"

"If they do," Peter replied wearily, "Mum'll have to divorce a zombie because she's about to kill him."

Caleb gazed out of the window, digesting the news. "But what are they arguing about anyway?"

"Mum's been offered a job in London. It's for loads more money than she can earn in Sheffield and it's for a top law firm, so she's chuffed to bits. But Dad's mightily annoyed because she didn't tell him that she was going for it."

"Because Dad would have said no, we're not moving to London, rar, rar, yadda yadda right from the start?" Caleb cottoned on quickly.

"Yep."

"Does this mean we've got to move to London? What about this coronavirus thing? Will we be actually allowed to move to London?"

"Don't know," Peter leaned heavily on the window frame, his fingers running through his hair. Neverminded the Coronavirus, or Covid-19 as everyone was calling it now, a move to a London school would put at least two hundred miles between him and Jake Webb.

"What the _!"

The boys looked at each other. In the middle of the shrieking wind, they suddenly heard an groaning that seemed to fill the bedroom. Peter felt a shiver shoot down his spine.

"It's a monster!" Caleb grabbed his brother in terror.

"There's no such things as monsters, Cay, come on! But what the heck is it?" With some difficulty he opened the window and stuck his head out.

The noise was coming from the row of poplars that usually stood proudly on the western edge of their garden, shielding the house from the worst of the weather. Now the trees bent double like courtiers bowing to the Queen as the gale howled through their branches.

But there was something else, something almost primeval, a noise that made their hair prickle, a grinding, teeth-on-edge sound that shook them to the core. Caleb stuck his head out to see for himself.

"Pete! It's the middle tree – it's coming down!"

Sure enough, one of the trees was behaving in a very odd manner. Peter and Caleb watched transfixed as the poplar bent towards them and then, like a nightmare in slow motion, continued to advance, its root system breaking out of the hillside with an ear-splitting cracking.

All at once Peter realised their danger. "Oh man! It's going to hit the roof!" He ducked back into his bedroom, dragging Caleb with him. Stopping only to scoop up the terrified cat, they dashed out of the room and down the stairs, diving hell-for-leather into the kitchen.

Their parents stopped arguing.

Immediately, above their heads, there was a massive crash as ten tonnes of poplar tree landed on the roof. With a scream, Caleb ducked under the table with Rascal. Peter clapped his hands to his ears to try to shut out the noise of falling slates and smashing glass. As the kitchen lights flickered, he watched his parents cling to each other, their fury forgotten. Peter ran over to them and they reached out and pulled him into their embrace.

They clung together desperately. Beneath the table Caleb could be heard tried to calm the cat.

For what seemed like hours the air was full of terrible noises and then, after a last huge shivery groan, it stopped. The house fell silent - the only sounds being the wind still howling outside and, rather ominously, running water. Mercifully, the kitchen lights had remained on.

They gazed at each other wide-eyed in shock. Eventually Mum found her voice.

"Please tell me that was nothing to do with our Caleb!"

CHAPTER 2

One Week Later

"I tell you, this place is ABSOLUTELY DEFINITELY HAUNTED! Look at them windows - the arch thingies above them look like EYEBROWS! It's like the whole house is a face – okay, more of a robot face than a ghost's, but still I can tell that it's NOT VERY PLEASED to see us and I'm NOT getting out of the car!"

Caleb pulled the car door shut and sat inside scowling.

"Ah the sweet tones of Cay! Just what we need to announce our arrival to our new neighbours." Dad, after a long journey in the car with a grumpy Caleb, sounded less like his usual patient self. Exasperated, he ran his hand through his thick greying hair, then looked up, surveying the stone facade of their new home.

"What do you reckon to it, Pete? I mean, I know it's a bit of an oddity, but it was available at short notice - and cheap cos it's next to a graveyard."

"I quite like it. I know what Cay means, but I don't think it's full of ghosts - more like it's full of memories cos it's so old. Anyway, he's just kicking off cos' he's got to share a room with me. Oh, there they are!"

"They" were Peter's beloved books, retrieved from the devastation of their old house and waiting to be unpacked in the new. Ignoring the sounds and rude gestures coming from within the car, Peter and Dad got to work and presently the downstairs rooms were full of boxes and cases, pot plants and Mum's Euphonium.

Caleb had steadfastly remained in the car. He had taken Rascal out from his travelling basket and held him in his arms as he addressed him.

"Rascal, you're going to be my ghost hunter. They say that cats can sense ghosts when humans can't. It's your job to make sure them smelly spooks don't come into our bedroom at night. No, don't go! Oh ouch!"

Rascal was generally of a friendly and tolerant nature but, after a journey confined in his basket, he shot out of Caleb's arms, scratching him in the process, and started to dart around the inside of the car, sticking his claws enthusiastically into the upholstery and Caleb.

"Dad, Razzy's mauling my arm!" Caleb opened the car door to wail to his father. Rascal shot out of the car, into the house and up the stairs, nearly tripping Peter up as he came out of the back bedroom.

Dad muttered something inaudible then cleared his throat. "Cay, given that you let Razzy out, get into the house now and find him. No, it's no good looking at me like that!"

Peter felt his phone buzz as he came downstairs. It was a WhatsApp message from Gran. For the past week, after their house had been ruined by the fallen tree, they had been staying with their grandparents. He quickly updated her, explaining how Mum had had to dash off to her new job as soon as they had arrived.

Leaving Yorkshire in the middle of the night, the Sat Nav had brought them into the East End through the intricate one-way system of the streets around Brick Lane. Caleb to his delight had learned some new swear words, which hadn't helped Mum's stress levels. Weirdly, despite all the busy-ness, the new house was on a quiet street, perched on the corner of a small square park and they could hear more birdsong than traffic noise.

A voice came from the kitchen. "Dad, can I go outside to the park?"

"Not on your own Cay. And it's a churchyard, not a park."

"But the back door leads straight out to it – so it's like our back garden. Please Dad - I'm totally bored in here!"

"I thought you were looking for Razzy?"

Dad went downstairs and found Caleb examining the back door at the end of the kitchen next to the bathroom. It did appear to lead out into the churchyard. A heavy metal key hung on a hook by the side of the door. Dad took it down and it fitted exactly. With a sharp crunching sound, the key turned, the door opened and daylight shone in. They wandered outside and stood in the sunshine, like chickens let out of their coop.

Peter came out to join them. "Cay's right, Dad. Technically this is all part of our garden. Please can we go and explore? We won't go out of the churchyard, and we can unpack later. Oh heck!"

A flash of ginger fur shot past them and ran off between the graves. Dad made a quick decision. "Right, you can go and explore and you can find that ruddy cat and bring him back. I'm staying here to carry on unpacking. Don't go out of the churchyard, remember these new Covid rules and stay two metres away from anyone you meet – and Cay, stick with Pete."

The pair walked slowly down the tree-lined pathway, past green-painted iron bins and park benches bearing brass plaques. Peter couldn't help thinking how cool it was – their own huge garden in the middle of all the houses and there was even enough room for a game of football. Just as he was thinking about this, he spotted a flash of ginger ahead of them.

"Pete - Razzy's disappeared into the church!" Caleb was jumping up and down excitedly. "We have the fastest cat in the WHOLE UNIVERSE. If they have races for cats, then Rascal would win it for sure!"

"Crap - the church must be open!" Peter stifled a nervous laugh as they crept through the doorway. The interior was brightly lit as the sun shone through tall windows that lined each wall. There was no sign of Rascal. "You take that side and I'll take this," he quickly told Caleb. "And let's be as quiet as possible in case anyone's around."

"Razzy! Ra…zzy! Razzy-razzy-rascal! Where are you, you daft cat?" Caleb prowled up the long line of pews whispering as loud as he dared. "Pete! There's no sign of him on this side of the church at all. Oh, don't say he's run up that weird staircase. I'm going to have to climb up to have a look."

"I think it's called a pulpit. Careful Cay, it all looks a bit high. Oh hello."

Peter was taken by surprise by the appearance of a plump blonde woman wearing a vicar's collar who appeared out of a side door, carrying Rascal. It seemed that Rascal had decided to behave, probably sensing that this was someone whom he could not mess about with.

"Is this your cat, per chance?" Her voice was brittle but friendly.

Peter blushed bright red and stepped back. "Yes he is. I'm really sorry. He got out by accident when we opened the back door."

"Oh, are you the boys who've moved into the Watch House? I thought you might be."

"Pete.. Peter.." Peter tried to ignore Caleb cooing in his right ear. "The Watch House? We live at No 1, Forest Close."

"Pete - she's a stranger, repeat, we're talking to a STRANGER…"

"Chill Cay, she's the vicar."

"But she's got our cat!"

"What d'you want me to do? Do karate on her or something?" He tried to focus on the woman. Rascal nestled in her arms, showing no signs of discomfort.

"Yes that's the Watch House. Built to house the watchmen

who watched over the churchyard at night with their blunderbusses to make sure no one tried to snatch a body." She smiled at them as though this was a perfectly normal thing to do.

"Really?"

"It's all in the parish records if you want to come over to look - we keep them in the vestry though you'd better come quick as it looks like we're going into this lockdown very soon doesn't it? Anyway - as I was saying, the reason your upstairs windows are so big and have such fine views over the churchyard, is so that the watchmen could keep an eye out for grave robbers. They got paid two guineas if they caught anyone, which must have been an absolute fortune back then."

She smiled broadly and then looked down at Rascal.

"Now, you lovely creature, do you want to go back to your masters? Come on then, off you go!" Gently, she passed the cat over to Peter. "I hope you settle in quickly - do ask your parents to call me if there's anything they need."

"Thanks Miss Er?"

"I'm the Rector here, the Reverend Louise Jamieson, but please call me Louise."

"Thanks – I'm Peter and he's Caleb, and, well you've met Rascal."

"Well good to meet you Peter and Caleb. I would shake hands with you, but, well you know the new rules!" She smiled ruefully and looked at her palms as if trying to inspect them for signs of virus.

They turned and walked back down the aisle.

"Oh boys!" There was a call from behind them.

"Yes?"

"Look out for the ghost!"

"Sorry?"

But, with a merry laugh, the Rector had disappeared back into her own quarters.

CHAPTER 3

At the Rector's warning, Caleb started to jump around as though he had ants in his pants, startling Rascal whose tail began to twitch.

"I knew it was haunted, I KNEW IT. I'm like a cat - got a sixth sense for knowing when there are ghosts around and I could tell the house was haunted as soon as I saw it!"

"Stop being an absolute idiot. She's just winding us up. I've told you a billion times that there's no such thing as ghosts."

Peter continued to tease his brother all the way across the churchyard until Caleb punched him so hard that the cat leapt out of his arms and bolted straight up into the large tree next to the house. Caleb put his tongue out at him and vanished through their back door.

"Oh crap!" With a groan, Peter clambered up the tree and attempted to coax the scared creature down. The tree was a chestnut, perfect for climbing and he saw it had a twin situated directly over the fence. But the cat was stuck there just out of his reach, as if superglued to the branch. He looked at Peter through big round eyes, like an owl who has been woken up in the daylight and is not very pleased about it.

"Come on puss!" Peter reached out to try and touch him. But the cat simply glared at him.

"Be like that then, you daft mog." Peter stopped trying and rested in the branches. He was now higher than his bedroom window and could see more of the churchyard which spread out before his eyes, unexpectantly green and spring-like amid the greyness of the East End. The church sat solidly in the middle of its churchyard – the Watch House situated at the south-west corner. Iron railings sealed the yard in on two sides

- along the western perimeter, interrupted by the main entrance to the churchyard, and along Forest Close. A solid wooden fence stretched straight across the eastern boundary up to the south-east corner of the church.

It suddenly dawned on him that he was content - he would not quite say happy, but quite definitely content. He was precisely one hundred and ninety-one miles away from Jake Webb. Big bonus. He felt that a door had opened in his life and he was about to step through it.

Deciding to abandon the cat to its fate, he climbed down and let himself back into the house, just in time to grab the last of the chocolate digestives that Dad had left out for elevenses.

That afternoon, while Dad waited in for the electrician, Peter went back to the churchyard having been challenged by Dad to find the oldest grave. Dragging a reluctant Caleb with him he decided that they should start with the graves on the side nearest their home. Here the graves were startlingly decrepit - in some cases he had to go right up to the stones to try to decipher the inscriptions with his fingers.

"There's one here dated 1751," he called over to his brother who was howling in pain having kicked a gravestone in frustration. Ignoring him, Peter carried on, now consulting his phone. "It says on the church website that the church was consecrated in 1746 - so this burial must have been one of the first but we might just find some earlier ones. Now what's this one?"

Caleb had stopped jumping around and was now sitting with his trainer off, nursing his poorly foot.

"Why are you asking me? Does this look like my "oh I'm so interested" face?"

"I said I'd play footy with you if you helped me check out the graves." Peter pointed out but it was no good. Caleb put his trainer back on and stood up.

"I'm going to have a look at what that JCB's doing."

To Peter's dismay, Caleb limped off towards the fence that ran along the eastern boundary. Beyond it, a snarling yellow digger was tearing up trees and bushes.

"Go and look at your stupid diggers! Peter called angrily at Caleb's disappearing back. "With you gone, the job's about a gazillion times quicker!" He continued to survey the graves, muttering to himself as he recorded the dates. "This one's 1751, this one's …erm, a bit hard to see…1763 - still they're all pretty early so I reckon we're in the right place. Oh here's one from 1747 – I'll make a note of it for Dad. Oh drat!" He started to feel drops of rain. He raced across the churchyard to where Caleb was peering over the fence, watching a JCB hard at work.

"Hey Cay, you coming in? It's raining." But Caleb was watching the digger.

"What do you reckon it's doing?"

"Who cares. Probably going to build new flats or something. Come on, you'll be soaked through."

Caleb was completely mesmerised by the mechanical brute. "You go. I'll come when it's finished this bit."

"Don't be too long. I'll be watching you from the house." Peter turned and dashed for home, the spring shower gaining in intensity as he ran.

Caleb stayed for a while, watching as the monster heaved and dragged the earth and battered down bushes as with a glorious ease of motion. Then it stopped and the driver climbed down from his cab. The magic abruptly ceasing, Caleb turned and started to walk towards the Watch House, only now realising how wet he was. He glanced up at his bedroom window and then broke into a run. Throwing himself in through the back door, Dad and Peter had to rapidly back away from his wetness. Rascal leaped out of his basket and fled upstairs.

"Caleb! Why didn't you come in when it started raining?"

"Dunno."

"Freak! I told you to come home with me. Oi! Dad, tell him to stop hitting me!!"

"Caleb, stop it. Go and get those wet clothes off. If you get a cold, your mum will think you've got Covid-19 and I'll be for it."

Caleb stomped off, dripping water all over the floor. As he started to climb the stairs he was nearly knocked off his feet by a yowling cat.

"What's got Razzy?" Peter had come out of the kitchen in time to see the petrified creature dash away into the lounge.

"Something's scared him I guess." Dad had followed them out.

Caleb halted on the third step, remembering something. "I reckon he's been scared by the man upstairs. What's he doing up there anyway - is he the electrician?"

Dad looked baffled. "What do you mean, Cay?"

"The man in our bedroom. I saw him looking out of the upstairs window at me as I came running in just now."

Peter and Dad exchanged glances. Dad came over to Caleb and put his arms around his shoulders.

"Cay, the electrician cancelled on us. He's coming tomorrow. There's not been anyone in the house except us."

"It's a ghost! The rector lady said this place was haunted!" Caleb wriggled out of his father's embrace and disappeared into the lounge after the cat.

Dad sighed and sat down wearily on the kitchen bench. "Crikey Norah! What are we going to do with him about this ghost stuff? I thought we'd leave it behind in Yorkshire but oh no."

"He's never going to sleep in our bedroom now," Peter pointed out.

Dad sighed. "Well, there's nowhere else so he'll have to. I

suppose he could sleep on the sofa down here, but he's already declared that the fireplace spooks him. Come on, let's go upstairs and make sure it isn't actually a burglar and pick up some dry clothes for him while we're up there." Ignoring the sounds of moving furniture coming from the lounge, they cautiously climbed the stairs and had a hasty look around. Both bedrooms were empty. Peter looked at Dad and shrugged.

Below them there was the sound of the front door opening.

"How did you get on?" Dad and Peter came running down to greet Mum as she came in, heavy laden.

"Well it's all very swish and they seem very nice people, but – well they've told me the office is closing tomorrow because of this Covid epidemic and we've all got to work from home. Here's all my kit." She gesticulated to a bulging laptop bag. "I reckon I'll need your help Pete to set it up."

"Cup of tea, love?"

"That would be great – I'm just going to check the Beeb to see what the latest is on this lockdown. All I'll say is thank God we moved yesterday otherwise we'd been stuck in Yorkshire. Oh you've done a grand job here, Tom – love the new shelves! But where's Cay?"

"Under the dining table."

"He saw a ghost." Peter added helpfully.

"Oh no, not again!"

Mum marched off to the lounge to find him. Dad put the kettle on. "Lockdown with a phantom in the house? Sometimes you just can't make Cay up!"

"Lockdown with a freakin' lunatic more like."

CHAPTER 4

Peter woke early when the sunlight streamed through the thin orange curtains, bathing the bedroom in a rosy glow. His watch showed that it was only eight o'clock, but he could hear the sound of sirens nearby. He crawled out of bed, went over to the window and opened the curtains.

Beyond the churchyard fence two police cars were parking by the entrance to the building site - a narrow lane that led to the site from the main road. The site was empty except for the JCB. From his lofty position, Peter watched as the police officers got out of their vehicles and walked into the site, to meet (at a respectful two-metre distance) a man in a high-vis jacket whom Peter guessed must be the JCB driver. There was an exchange of conversation and then the man led them behind the JCB, clearly to see something.

Peter grabbed his clothes and began to get dressed.

"Cay!"

"Huh?"

(Mum had eventually persuaded Caleb to go to sleep in his own bed after promising him that Rascal could sleep in the bedroom too in case the ghost came back, and that hot milk and honey would guarantee that he would sleep through until morning.)

"Get dressed. There's something happening with your JCB!"

Peter was halfway across the churchyard before he heard the back door open behind him and Caleb come racing out. They ran over and hung on the fence, straining to hear what was going on. The police officers had gone back to their cars. One car drove away immediately but in the other the boys could see a policewoman talking into a radio.

The JCB driver was staring disconsolately at something beyond his machine while he smoked a cigarette. Then he kicked one of the JCB's wheels and turned and started walking towards them, jumping in surprise when he realised that they were watching.

"What you staring at?"

"What's going on?" Peter asked politely.

"Nothing for noseys, imps or bogies."

"Is the JCB a 2CX or a 3CX?" Caleb was still studying the machine. The man's hard glare softened.

"Only 2CX. It's a small site. The 3CX would be far too big. Could have done with a 1CX really but there weren't any available. You know your diggers, son."

"I love JCBs. Want to be a digger driver when I'm older."

"I'd invite you round for a go but I can't really do that today." The man nodded sadly in the direction of the police car.

"What are they doing here?"

"I've found a ruddy skeleton - no, don't get too excited, it looks really old and there's some sort of gravestone so it doesn't look like anyone's been murdered. The trouble is that it means I can't finish the job today and we're on a bloomin' tight schedule as the boss wants this site ready as soon as possible." The man lit another fag. "The police are calling for their forensics people to check it out and even if it is just an old burial, as they reckon, they'll then have to call the blasted archaeologists in to do their excavating. And me and Mildred will be stuck here doing nothing!"

"Mildred?"

"The 2CX. Lovely girl she is too. Comfy seat and air con in summer. Wish I could show you."

The man looked so gloomy that Peter felt rather sorry for him. "What does the gravestone say?"

"I wrote it down, hang on." He stamped the end of his fag out on the ground and started to rummage through his pockets. "Here you go." He withdrew a tatty piece of paper. "S'not much. I'll read it out to you as I'm not supposed to come near you, am I, with this social-distancing thing going on." He started to read: "'WILLIAM WADSWORTH 1795' – the stone's propped up against that wall but it's not much to look at. There's nothing else on it, no cross or anything. Oh, look sharp - the Sweeny's back."

He stuffed the paper back in his pocket and began to walk over to meet the police. Caleb climbed down from his perch, his face white and anxious.

"Can we go back now?"

"Okay. I don't think there's much else to see at the moment. We'll be able to see from the house when the forensics people arrive."

They walked back across the churchyard, Peter noting that Caleb kept glancing up at their bedroom window. Suddenly he had a thought.

"Don't you think it's weird that someone would be buried in a bit of waste ground when there's a great big churchyard right next door?"

"Not really. Maybe they didn't go to church."

"I don't think it was quite like that in those days," Peter started to speak but realised that his brother wasn't listening and had dashed into the sanctuary of their home.

Forensics must have come and gone while Dad took them to the barbers for their "just in case they close all the barber shops we don't want you two looking like scarecrows" haircut. After lunch, with their hair neatly cropped, they ran back to the fence. Peering over it they found a solitary woman. Wearing a blue hard hat and orange high-vis jacket, she was staring at the ground with a trowel and a tape measure in her hands and a worried look on her face.

"What's up?" Peter called over to her.

She turned in surprise. "What are you boys doing here?"

"We live here." Peter found that he was starting to enjoy saying it. The woman brightened.

"Could do me a favour and run and fetch the vicar?"

"D'you mean the Rector. Sure – but why?"

"I've got to remove this skeleton. The rules say that a witness should be present when human remains are removed from a site. And I need to find somewhere suitable to keep him til we find an alternative resting place." She spoke very fast as though what she had to do was of the greatest urgency.

"Him?"

"The man in the grave. Forensics have confirmed he's a male in his twenties. They're not going to do any further testing because they've concluded that the state of the body is compatible with the date on the gravestone. Not brilliant science but they've got two people self-isolating and are a bit stretched. Now, could you go and knock on the door of the vicarage or rectory, or whatever it is called, and see if he's in please."

"She."

"Ah yes, see if *she's* in, and if she isn't, see if there's a phone number or something for her. I'd go myself but I've so much to do here, it isn't funny."

The boys raced across to the Rectory, which was across the street from the main entrance to the churchyard. The Rector was in, and grabbed her boots and coat as soon as they explained the situation. She left them to walk up the main road to join the archaeologist on site while the boys dashed across the churchyard, back to their old position by the fence.

"She's coming now!" Peter told the archaeologist, who was

looking considerably happier. She smiled and thanked them and then hurried off to meet the Rector.

"Yuck, I don't like the idea of skeletons."

"It's a churchyard you idiot. There are skeletons all over the place."

Caleb whimpered and hung on the fence, making sure his feet were well off the ground.

Peter suddenly had an idea. "Hey - maybe it's your ghost?"

"Huh?"

"The skeleton. Maybe it's your ghost - the one you reckon you saw yesterday in our room. Makes sense - that's when the digger would have disturbed his grave."

"Shut up about ghosts. Dad told you to not to tease me about it."

"I'm not teasing you - I'm taking you seriously for once! Oi, stop it!"

"Ow! I'm telling Dad!"

"Shurrup – they're coming!"

The archaeologist was talking very fast and loudly to the Rector.

"So, as I say, Historic England state that one should ideally leave the remains in the ground, however this is not an option here as the developers want the work on this site to restart tomorrow, so I was going to ask you to help us in the removal and then we can transfer the remains to the church before we get a decision on reburial. And while we've still got the chance before all these lockdown restrictions come in."

"In the church? You want me to keep the bones in the church?" The Rector sounded concerned.

"Only until we get a report from the police to say that they are not treating this as a crime scene. Then we can rebury the body in your churchyard. Don't worry - the developers will have to pay for it - you might even be able to claim storage costs."

Peter could see that the Rector was not convinced.

"Look - I'm happy to take it, but I'll just need a minute to find a suitable place. And how are we going to carry the skeleton over? Can we manage - the two of us?"

"These boys may be able to help – do you know their parents?"

Peter found his voice. "I'd love to help, but my brother won't be allowed as it'll give him nightmares."

"Well, we will have to ask your parents first. Are they at home?"

"Yes - shall I go and ask them?"

The Rector looked up. "Actually, why don't I come with you? I need to go into the church to work out where we could store it."

Peter nudged Caleb. They walked back towards the Watch House, waiting for the Rector to join them, Caleb doing a jittery dance which made him look like he needed the loo.

"You alright?"

"Dunno – I just feel a bit weird. It's like we've done something really naughty."

CHAPTER 5

As Peter expected, Mum's first reaction was a big N.O. Aware of the Rector's presence, she and Dad had a whispered argument.

"There's no way on earth that Caleb is to see the skeleton - he'll be having nightmares for weeks!

"But you could help. I could take Cay for a walk out of the way. Pete could be useful to them and he'd find it really interesting." Mum looked at her husband, fizzing with exasperation and then harrumphed, realising she had lost.

Dad went off with Cay to do some shopping (with Mum's instructions ringing in their ears to keep well away from any graveside). Meanwhile Peter and Mum followed the Rector to the building site. The Rector was still fussing about where she could hide a skeleton and wondering whether it could fit in the room where she kept the Christmas Market equipment. By the time they arrived at the site, the archaeologist had laid out the remains neatly in a plastic casket to the side of the hole.

Keeping a healthy distance from her, Peter took a photo of the grave and then of the gravestone.

The archaeologist seemed very excited to see them and started talking again, almost without taking a breath. "Very neat job actually - no evidence whatsoever of any other archaeological remains around the grave. And look here." She held out a Tupperware box towards them which contained some small rusty objects. "Can you see the hinges and metal work of the original coffin? This metal clasp which would have been used to hold it shut – it's in the form of a rose. This shows that they buried him with real care and attention. But why here outside the churchyard? Non-conformist? Jewish?"

The Rector looked puzzled. "There were plenty of Jewish

cemeteries around here in 1795, and likewise for the non-conformist community and the Catholics too. No - this chap looks like he'd fallen out with the Church of England, and pretty seriously I'd say, to be buried in unconsecrated ground!"

"Suicide?" This was from Mum.

The adults looked at one another and then at Peter. He had been trying to take a photo of the skeleton itself. Feeling rather guilty, he shoved his phone away.

"Quite possibly," said the Rector, a little too dismissively. "Now, are we ready to move him? Do I have to recite the funeral service or anything?"

"No - just make sure we carry him in a dignified way."

"Well, I do think a prayer would be nice to set us off," the Rector proposed.

"Fine." The archaeologist was in no mood to argue. "Now, if Peter could carry the feet-end, Peter's mum, the head-end and the Rector and I will keep away from you both. Shouldn't be too heavy. Over to you Reverend!"

The Rector stepped back from the skeleton and called out the bidding prayer from the funeral service. Mum and Peter took their positions and then stood still, listening to the words as they were proclaimed loud and clear in the silent yard.

"I am the Resurrection and the Life. He who believes in me shall not die but shall have eternal life!"

Peter shivered at the age-old words - maybe Caleb was not the only one to be touched by the weirdness. He picked up his end of the casket and saw, with healthy respect, how Mum picked up the end with the grinning skull. The casket was surprisingly heavy - probably because many of the bones were still wrapped in the earth that had cherished them for so long. Peter figured that they might start rattling around if the earth was removed completely.

They made their solemn procession down the lane to the main road, turning left down the street passing all the shops and houses catching some odd looks from the few passers-by. Turning left again they processed round and through the gate into the churchyard. The Rector unlocked the church door and they went in and walked up the nave to the chancel, placing the bones in front of the altar.

"Nicely done," said the archaeologist after they had all stepped back.

"I'm afraid it can't stay in this spot," the Rector spoke up. "Even though the church building might be closing up for this lockdown, I've still got a wedding in the diary for Saturday week…"

Peter noticed something.

"Can you put him over there." He pointed to a sepulchre bearing the effigy of a knight which was positioned along the north wall. "I reckon there's room behind that tomb."

He and the R went over to look.

"You're absolutely right, Peter. No one will see it behind Sir Percy."

"Who's Sir Percy?"

"Sir Percival FitzGerald? Oh he was a crusader knight from the family who owned all the land around here. The story goes that he was travelling back from the Holy Land - where he'd been fighting with the Crusader armies to take Jerusalem back from the Saracens. He'd disembarked and was travelling home to Bethnal Green across the wastes of the Isle of Dogs when a wild dog attacked him. His horse threw him and he was badly injured but he fought on until he came to the old parish church at Stepney. He was so exhausted that he collapsed and died in the church narthex, but in doing so, he crushed the dog. So they built a large tomb for him and the legend was born. Then the old church was destroyed in the Blitz, hence we've adopted him."

"Oh right." As they stowed the casket out of sight, Peter had an absurd thought of Granny's dog Spike, a valiant little Yorkie, taking on a knight in armour and tried not to smile. But the Rector had not finished.

"Here's a book all about the history of the church - it was written by one of our parishioners who's a professor of history at King's College. You're welcome to have it. Tells you all about the legend of Sir Percy and the Hound."

"Thanks very much." He smiled and clasped the book to his chest. He'd had an idea.

"Are you ready Pete?" Mum was calling. They said goodbye and wandered home, Peter eager to start reading. They found Dad and Caleb in the kitchen having been to the supermarket. Dad was putting the kettle on.

"We saw your procession from the front bedroom," Caleb told them. "You looked a bit funny, the five of you being so serious."

"You can't count, Cay." Mum pointed out as she took her shoes off. "There were Peter and me, the Rector and the archaeologist. That's four, not five."

"No, that's not true. There was you and Pete carrying the box, the Rector out in front, then the archaeologist, and behind her was the man in the funny hat. That's five." Caleb held his fingers out and marked off each one.

Mum looked up at him. "Cay, there was no man there."

"Oh ssssssugar!"

Caleb dashed out of the kitchen to his hiding place under the dining table. As if he could understand English, Rascal leaped out of his basket to go to join him. Mum sighed and ran her hands through her hair.

"What the heck are we going to do with him. This is getting downright daft!"

CHAPTER 6

Peter realised that it was one of those moments that if he sat very quietly, his parents would forget he was there. He was sitting at the kitchen table reading the church history book - which was way more interesting than he had expected. He had just got to the part where a new rector had arrived to find the church warden up to no good. Stealthily he turned the pages, keeping one ear open from anything he might learn.

Mum and Dad were in deep discussion. Caleb was in the lounge asleep on the sofa with Rascal to guard him. (Mum had loudly declared the room to be a ghost-free zone, while circling the room and banging the frying pan.)

"So, we really have to do something about Cay and these ghosts, Tom."

"I was hoping it might stop when we moved down here." Dad had made the tea and passed his wife a steaming mug.

"Yeah - maybe it wasn't the best idea to get a house next to a graveyard then." She took the tea and muttered thanks.

"Oh Lizzy, we've been through all that. Until I get a job, we've got no chance of renting a better place around here, even with your new salary. We've got all the repairs on the old house to pay for before we can think of selling it. And with this Covid-19 virus and the schools supposed to be shutting, I can't start looking for work if the boys are going to be stuck at home. The rent on this place is really low and it's fine - it's just a bit draughty."

"And haunted."

"Now not necessarily in the house. Cay saw the ghost in the street today."

Mum snorted as she sipped her tea. "Oh, don't you start.

There're no such things as ghosts. He's just got a very strange imagination - he's been watching too many films."

(Peter recalled how Caleb had got this thing in his head about ghosts after he saw a film at a birthday party about a kid who saw dead people everywhere.)

Dad brightened up. "Why don't we have a chat with the vicar lady? She seemed sensible enough."

"The Rector you mean? I don't know Tom, it's all a bit embarrassing."

"Well look, we can't take him to the GP about this when they're tied up treating all the people who are ill with Covid-19. The Church is supposed to be able to deal with ghosts isn't it?"

Mum looked alarmed. "Do you mean exorcism? That's a bit extreme – Caleb's not possessed. Now the cat might be, I'll admit."

Dad smiled reassuringly. "Not exorcism. But she might just be able to talk to him, reassure him and make him feel better."

Peter signed as a thrill of fear shot through him. Noticing him for the first time, Mum rounded on him like a dog on a scent.

"What are you smiling at?"

"Nothing Mum. I'm just reading my book." He gestured at the page in front of him.

"If this is one of your wind ups, then I'm not impressed." Mum's frustration clearly had reached boiling point.

"Lizzie, I really don't think Pete's got anything to do with it?" Dad moved quietly over to his wife and drew her into his arms.

"Well, for the good of his health he'd better not have!" But the rage had gone and Mum, now looking terribly worn out, rested her head on Dad's shoulder.

Peter suddenly felt dreadfully sorry for her and wondered if it had really been a wise move to come down to London.

CHAPTER 7

Razzy-Razzy-Rascal - you and me are okay here sleeping down here aren't we, now Mum's made it GHOST-PROOF. I don't mind that it's the room nearest to the boiler and it makes a strange MOANING noise when it comes on. It's nice and warm and cosy and snug under here – just how you like it…

Oh, hang on cat, Mum's calling me.

NO! I'm NOT going to talk to the lady vicar. That's the MOST STUPIDEST idea I've ever heard IN THE WORLD!!! She'll think I'm BONKERS. No I am not!

NOOOOOO!!!

Well she'll have to DRAG me out of here then. I'm going to attached myself with Gorilla Glue to the table legs so if they DO want to get me out of here, they'll have to call the FIRE BRIGADE!!!!!!!!!!!!!!!!!!!!!!!!!!!!

CHAPTER 8

If the Reverend Jamieson was at all surprised to find her parishioner hiding in the farthest corner of the lounge beneath the dining table, barricaded in by dining chairs and a cat basket, she did not show it. She dropped down onto her knees and peered under the table to see where Caleb actually was, and then she sat back and gazed at a print of a Picasso on the wall.

"I've seen a ghost you know."

There was a strange noise from under the table - the sort of noise a cat might make if it was being hugged too hard for its own liking.

"It was when I was at theological college. I was in the refectory reading – that's what we called the dining hall - we could work in there when it wasn't being used for meals - when I saw a woman in an old-fashioned servant costume walk in the door, move across the room and out through the wall."

Another squeak.

"The thing was that it was all so normal and so definitely unspooky that it was only after a few minutes I realised that she must have been a ghost. You see, the college staff didn't tend to be able to walk through walls."

At this point an extremely annoyed cat shot out from under the table, narrowly missing her.

"Was that Rascal?"

"Isssss"

"He's gorgeous – or at least he was. He's completely vanished. Can he see the ghost too?"

Silence.

"So what I'm trying to say is that you're not crazy or anything like that. I wasn't joking when I told you that this Watch House was haunted – there have been rumours of a ghost here for years."

A head poked out from under the tablecloth.

"So other people have seen him?"

The Rector looked down at the scared face.

"If it's the same man, yes. Now listen. Your mum has made you some hot chocolate. Come on out and drink it with me. If I sit over in that big pink chair, we should be far enough apart for social distancing. Now I want to tell you a little bit that I know about ghosts - and then I want to know all about your ghost because I think I might be able to help."

"I don't need any help!" The boy emerged from under the table and took his hot chocolate.

"I'm not talking about you." The Rector looked thoughtful. "Now, from what I've learned, there appear to be several types of ghosts. One kind is like my servant lady I saw back at college. She doesn't seem to be aware of the modern world, she just follows the same route she took in life, including walking through doors that once existed but now don't. Well, I think her presence is like a film recording – it just keeps playing back on loop if you see what I mean. Can I tell you another thing?"

Caleb gulped his drink nervously and nodded.

"A while back a parishioner of mine died - lovely old chap, and for a while I had to look after his dog while we were finding it a new home. One evening I was watching a video of a church concert in which Albert – that was the old man's name - had performed a song. When the video showed Albert singing, the dog went bananas. The dog could see and hear Albert but couldn't smell him – and I think the dog knew in its heart that Albert had died. But the dog couldn't understand the technology involved in playing back the video of his master and was rather rattled by it."

"So I think that seeing ghosts like my servant lady could be some natural phenomenon that we don't understand, but that we can be no more harmed by them than by a video recording."

Caleb looked puzzled. "But my ghost wasn't like that. He did look as though he was wanting to tell me something."

"Do you feel like you can tell me what he looked like?"

The boy was starting to relax. He screwed his eyes up and thought for a moment.

"He's much younger than Dad, but he looks worried and sad which makes him look older. He's thin and going a bit bald and he's wearing a right long coat like the one Mum has, with buttons running all the way down. He's got shoes with a buckle and he's wearing a floppy three-sided hat. Oh and he's got a belt with what looks like a football rattle stuck in it."

He finished rather breathlessly.

"I'm very impressed by your powers of observation, Caleb. I reckon your ghost might be from the same time in history as the skeleton in the grave - but we mustn't jump to conclusions. The football rattle is interesting. I've got a notion that I know what sort of person might carry one - I think I'll have to do a bit of research."

"Can you make him go away and never come near me again?" Caleb spoke with a hint of desperation.

"Well, this is the problem. I think your sort of ghost is wandering the earth because his soul is unsettled. Something has gone wrong - his soul should be able to pass through straight to Heaven, but it can't. Now the first thing to do is to go to the place where he initially appeared to you - your bedroom wasn't it? We can say a prayer to calm his restless spirit down. Do you think we can ask your mum to come upstairs with us?

Caleb thought for a moment and then nodded. "What's the

second thing?"

"The second thing is for you and your brother to find out as much as you can about who he was in life so we can work out what he wants."

"Can't we just bury the skeleton in the churchyard. I'm nearly one hundred percent positive that it's the ghost's and that's what he wants!"

"Not as easy as that, I'm afraid. I'd have to get permission from the Church Council - and it's a bit tricky because the churchyard here is officially full of bodies - even if most of them have now been reduced to their bones. And the police still haven't confirmed that they are not going to investigate the body."

"Do you mean they still think it's someone who was murdered?"

"Not quite. More likely it means they haven't had time to fill in the form to say they're sure the body is too old to have been murdered."

Caleb was now interested. "But what if he <u>was</u> murdered two hundred years ago?"

"Now that's for us to find out!"

CHAPTER 9

Razzy – Razzy Rascal - it's all okay now. The Rector lady person turned out to be really nice and she DEFINITELY believes me AND she's seen ghosts too, which makes her super cool.

So me and her and Mum go upstairs to my bedroom and Mum and me sit on my bed, and the Rector stands at the other side of the room. She lights a candle and sticks it on Pete's desk and then gets us to put our hands together. And then she says this prayer thing:

"Dear Lord," she says, "please look after this unfortunate soul who for some reason appears to be restless upon this earth. Please give him your peace and the reassurance of everlasting life united with you in Heaven. And please comfort Caleb…"

"And Rascal" I say…

"And Rascal, so that they are no longer afraid. And please give us the strength and wits to work out why this spirit is so troubled. We ask this is Jesus's name. Amen."

"AMEN" I shout loudly cos I reckon God's probably a BIT DEAF cos he's so old. And Mum murmurs "Amen" too and it's OVER.

And it's all a bit weird, but okay really and Mum looks at me and SMILES and squeezes my hand.

The Rector says she'll leave the candle here though I should ONLY light it if my parents say I can, and NEVER LEAVE A LIT CANDLE ALONE.

Then she goes. Mum asks me how I feel and I say that I am actually feeling a lot better – and it's true. It's like the feeling you have after you've had to do something scary - like read in Assembly, and it's gone OKAY and you didn't MUCK IT UP.

Anyway, I'm glad the ghost has gone away cos tomorrow lockdown is OFFICIALLY STARTING. Our new schools are closed (WOO HOO!!!!) Even Perfect Pete is pleased about this cos it is a bit scary going to school in a new place. Mum's got to work from home and we're only allowed out ONCE A DAY for exercise. I don't need exercise as I'm SUPER FIT already so I've told Dad he can have my slot as he needs it cos he's got a fat belly.

Dad says that if I keep up those remarks, I'll be lucky to survive lockdown...

CHAPTER 10

The first day of lockdown was not going well.

"Why've I got to do history? I hate history! Why can't I do a project on tractors or JCBs – yeah JCBs cos I know shed loads about them?"

Caleb was really testing Dad's patience.

"We've been through all this, Caleb. This project is a nice bit of detective work – and it's to help you, you daft chump! You heard what the Rector said - that it's our job to work out who the ghost was."

Peter figured that Dad was regretting appointing himself official home-school headmaster. He had spent breakfast going on at length about getting himself a proper teacher's jacket with arm patches and a pipe, until Caleb had threatened to drown himself in his Coco Pops.

Mum was already crazily busy with her new job. She had set up her computer in the tiny room next to the kitchen that she called the pantry, and that had been the last they had seen of her all morning.

"Come on Cay," Peter tried to help Dad out. "Remember we think that the ghost could be the skeleton, William Wadsworth, or he might be one of the names on the gravestones in the churchyard. So, as it's the obvious place to start, we're going to make a list of the names on the gravestones so we can check them out."

Caleb made a rude gesture at his brother. Peter gave up being helpful and went back to his book, shovelling Shreddies into his mouth as he read.

Caleb went back to arguing. "But why can't Pete do it on his own? He's such a total nerd, he loves history and all that!"

Dad was getting cross.

"Because your job is to go round the churchyard with me and make a list of all the people who died around the same time William did."

Giving up, Dad turned to Peter.

"Good book Pete?"

Peter nodded. "Yes - I figured it might help us with your ghost Cay - that's why I borrowed it. And it is actually interesting - in 1809 there's this new rector appointed – a man called Joshua King - and he's discovered that the church warden, who's called Joseph Merceron, has been up to all sorts of dodgy stuff like paying the collection money to his mates. There's also something here about the watchmen in the Watch House. Says they were claiming off the Parish for the capture of non-existent body snatchers and paying the money over to Merceron!"

"Bloomin' heck! Exciting times eh!" Dad was impressed. "And you say history's boring, our Cay! NO, you're not unpacking the PS4 - I told you, you're coming to help me this morning!"

"But I want to play Fortnite!!" Caleb yelled back from the corner by the back door where he had discovered all the boxes that were still to be unpacked.

"You can't play Fortnite. You're far too young!"

Peter sighed. All was lost. Caleb had trapped Dad into the "You're-too-young-for-Fortnite" row that had been raging on and off since Caleb was in Year 2. This was an argument that Caleb could happily keep going for hours if you let him. He got up from the table crossly and stomped over to switch the radio off. Dad and Caleb, surprised, shut up.

"Listen to this: 'The Reverend King described how he was petitioned by those who had suffered from Merceron's regime of corruption' So, as I was saying - of all the people who were coming to moan about Merceron, there's this woman who reckoned he'd accused her son of a crime he didn't do and the kid had ended up being executed for it. It says here: *'during Merceron's corrupt reign, her son, Nathaniel Daykin, had been tried and found guilty of murdering a watchman while being apprehended for body-snatching. He was hung on his fourteenth birthday'.*"

"And?" muttered Caleb sulkily.

"He might be your ghost."

Quiet descended on the kitchen as they mulled this idea over.

"Could be," Dad cautiously admitted as he chewed on a piece of toast.

"My ghost looked older," Caleb told them reaching for the milk to pour over his second bowl of Coco Pops. "And I thought the ghost was the skeleton, William Wadsworth."

"We don't know that for sure," Dad reminded him, "we've got to keep an open mind. Anyway, how about we go and see if Nathaniel's buried in the churchyard?"

"That's if they allowed criminals to be buried on sacred land," Peter pointed out.

"What's sacred land?" Caleb asked.

"In England it's land that's been blessed by the church so that people can be buried there," Peter told him. "It comes from the old Christian idea that people's remains rest in peace waiting for the end of time, but they reckon it also came about for public health reasons to make sure dead bodies didn't pollute the water supply and things like that."

"The unbaptised, suicides and lunatics." Mum had come out of the pantry to put the kettle on. They looked up at her. "Not allowed to be buried in a churchyard – that was the law back then. I reckon that that would rule out most of the population around here now. Would you believe that the Church of England only changed the rules in 2007!" She shook her head. "Now, are you lovely lot going outside or what? It's really sunny out there."

"I'm staying here working," Peter told her. "Dad and Cay are going out to examine all the graves."

"Well get going, I need some peace and quiet as I've got a meeting starting in five minutes with the senior partner." With that Mum disappeared back into the pantry.

So Dad and Caleb, armed with notepad and pencil, went out into the churchyard and Peter remained at the breakfast table reading the book the Rector had given him, occasionally jotting something down. Murmurs of noise came from behind the pantry door - Mum's meeting had started. Other than that it was peaceful, and from outside the window, he could hear a blackbird singing loudly to its mate.

As he worked, he gradually became aware of someone else in the room. He looked up puzzled. Dad and Caleb had not come back in and he could still hear Mum's voice coming through the pantry door.

Then he froze.

A man was standing silently in the doorway of the kitchen that led to the stairs. Peter stared at him, feeling the hairs on his arms stand on end. He could not see the face of the man too well – the light from the window over the stairs was behind him, but he could make out the strange clothes he was wearing - a long dark jacket down to the knees with a double row of buttons down the front, a white shirt with a grubby grey scarf, a thick black belt around the coat with an odd wooden rattle shoved into the belt like a gun-holster. He was so real and yet not – Peter could just make out the outline of the letter box in their front door through the figure's chest - and it gave him a very strange feeling.

Was he scared? That was the odd thing - no he was not. The man did not look in the least bit threatening - but Peter found himself filled with a vivid sense of sadness.

"You all right mate?" Peter found his voice, hideously loud as it boomed around the kitchen. The vision vanished.

"Oh man!" Peter rocked back on his chair and put his hands through his hair, realising he was drenched with sweat. Then, remembering his job, he grabbed his pen and notebook and made a quick sketch of the vision.

While he was doing it, Mum came out of her den.

"You okay love? I thought I heard you talking to someone?"

"Mum" Peter looked up at her, pale and excited. "I've seen the ghost – and it's a watchman!"

CHAPTER 11

Razzy-Razzy-Rascal, this is so UNBELIEVABLY unfair!

When it was just me and you who saw the ghost then it' was "shut up Caleb" or 'don't be stupid' or 'let's get the Rector in to say a prayer and EXORCISE Caleb cos Caleb's a FREAKIN' fruitcake' yadder yadder YADDER!

But when PERFECT PRETTY PETER sees him, it's "oh that's INCREDIBLY interesting" and "oh it's soooo FASCINATING that it's a watchman" and they believe him STRAIGHT AWAY even though it's only him who saw it and he might be COMPLETELY AND UTTERLY lying through his twisted BRACE-COVERED teeth!?!

(But he probably isn't lying cos Pete is too ultra-BORING to lie.)

It makes me TOTALLY AND ABSOLUTELY raving mad the treatment I get in this house. I'm going to phone the NSPCC, I will really!

Oh, I forgot. I can't even do that because them ROTTEN STINKERS won't even BUY me a phone. It's like I'm trapped in the SIXTEENTH century.

In fact the only two people in the KNOWN UNIVERSE who haven't got phones are the Watchman ghost (cos he was alive before phones were invented) and ME (cos my parents are just the lamest, rubbishest most PATHETIC parents EVER invented).

So I'm going to launch an OFFICIAL sulk. I'm going to stay up here with you and I'm not going to budge. And even if the ghost does appear again, then I DON'T CARE!!!!

CHAPTER 12

"So, a watchman. How did you figure that out?" Dad was peering at the sketch in Peter's notebook. It was late morning and Dad and Mum were in the kitchen enjoying a quick coffee - Dad having finally got the expresso machine unpacked and working to Mum's absolute delight. Peter was sticking white paper to one of the kitchen walls so that they could record their findings.

"It's actually this that really proved it." Peter pointed to the rattle stuck in the man's belt. "I've been doing a bit of research and these rattles were carried by watchmen in the eighteenth century so they could make loads of noise to summon other watchmen. It was before whistles were invented. And we know of course that watchmen lived in this house."

"Did you find Nathaniel's grave?" Mum supped her coffee, interested.

"Nope - and we had a proper good look. But I've been thinking - it doesn't really mean anything because Nathaniel could be buried at any churchyard around here. According to Google Maps, they're all over the place in London cos there's a church on just about every street. Or he might even have been buried in the prison. And we know that Nathaniel was definitely not a watchman. I mean - he was only fourteen and he was executed for killing a watchman."

"Perhaps there's a record at the diocesan office as to who's buried where. Oh heck - is that the time!" Mum jumped up and grabbed her coffee and went back into her pantry.

Peter was Googling 'diocesan office' when a thought struck him. "Hang on. What if our ghost is the watchman who Nathaniel what's-his-name murdered?"

"And William Wadsworth was that watchman?" Dad was taken with this idea.

The door of the pantry swung open once more.

"But why would a murdered man be buried outside the churchyard?" Mum was eavesdropping again.

"I thought you had work to do," Dad told her. She huffed and retreated back inside.

Just then the landline rang. They looked at each other, startled, as it was the first time that it had rung since they had moved in. Dad realised he should answer it. Peter listened briefly to Dad's rather sparse side of the conversation but soon went back to his papering.

A figure appeared in the kitchen - it was Caleb, his official sulk apparently over, summoned by the unusual sound. Dad's conversation finished and he replaced the receiver.

"That was the Rector," he announced, sounding rather bewildered. She's rung to warn us that she's locking the churchyard gates because of the lockdown, but she's no problem with us using the yard ourselves and she's asked us to keep an eye on the church in case of vandalism."

Dad paused, trying to remember the next part of the message. "Oh, she then mentioned the skeleton and told me that there are plans to re-inter the body where it was found – that means rebury it," he added quickly in answer to Caleb's quizzical look. "It looks like the archaeologist was a bit too hasty in taking it out and the developer seems to think they can build over the grave in a way that doesn't damage it. And the final thing is that she reckons Caleb's ghost might be that of a watchman."

"No!" cried Caleb in anguish.

"But we thought it was a watchman," said Dad, slow on the uptake.

"I meant burying him back in his grave! He needs to be buried in the churchyard – on scared ground or whatever you said it was called!"

"Sacred ground," Peter prompted him. "This is all a bit sudden, Dad. Did she say why?"

"Nothing particularly mysterious. The churchyard doesn't have any spare burial plots – any funerals these days take the remains to the City of London Cemetery which is way out east. She told me that to bury our skeleton in the churchyard would need permission from the Church Council and they won't grant it unless there's an extremely good reason, because they've been saying no to burials here for the past seven years.

She also said that the skeleton is to remain where it is until she gets the letter from the police confirming that they're not investigating and then it's going back in. She reckoned it wouldn't be long now as she figures the developer is now putting pressure on the police so that building work can start up again."

"But the Rector told me that his spirit was restless and he needed to be buried in the churchyard!"

"She didn't quite say that, Cay." Mum had obviously been listening again from behind her door and reappeared in the kitchen. "We've still no real connection between who the ghost might be and the skeleton. The Rector mentioned that this place had a reputation of being haunted long before the grave was opened."

"That could be simply because the house looks like it must be haunted," Peter pointed out reasonably.

"But he's GOT to be buried in the churchyard - or he's going to KEEP HAUNTING ME!" Caleb ran out of the room once more, the tears streaming down his face.

"I've got to get back to work," Mum announced to her now rather sceptical audience. "Tom," she gave her husband a look which suggested that he was entirely responsible for the whole episode, "I think you should light the Rector's candle for him to calm him down."

With this she disappeared. Dad went out of the room muttering grumpily to himself. Peter picked up a black marker and wrote on the wall:

INVESTIGATION

Who was William Wadsworth?

Why was he buried outside the churchyard?

WW's date of death 1795 = the period when Merceron the church warden was doing lots of illegal stuff. Is there a link?

Is there a link between WW and Nathaniel Daykin? ND was executed several years before 1809 – when as this around 1795? Did he know WW? Did he murder WW?

Who is our ghost? ND? WW?

Then he had another thought and quickly scribbled:

Someone else? Another watchman who was murdered by ND?

They needed answers and fast!

CHAPTER 13

Razzy-Razzy-Rascal this lockdown thing is WAY TOO WEIRD. The churchyard is now COMPLETELY LOCKED UP with chains twisted all over the gates and big signs stuck on the black railings saying that the church is closed – if it wasn't ENTIRELY OBVIOUS! Dad is being TOTALLY CRINGE and taking photos of everything saying it's FOR POSTERITY and that we're living through a 'unique period of history', or something like that.

And you're not allowed to go out - except to get essentials like CAT FOOD of course - Mum said that Grandad got busted the other day trying to go fishing. He told the cops that he was trying to get food for his poor little dog who was wasting away (which is DEAD FUNNY cos Spikey has got a belly on him that's the size of Sheffield!) and they let him OFF.

But Dad and me went to Tescos and it was TOTALLY STRANGE - we had to wait for ages and ages to go in and there was white tape on the pavement LIKE PARKING SPOTS showing where you had to stand to keep away from people.

And when we got in there was loads of empty shelves and ABSOLUTELY NO BOG ROLL as people have been panic-buying it – which I really don't get - I mean does Covid-19 make you POO a lot?

There are practically NO CARS going up our road which is completely strange and someone has turned UP THE VOLUME on the birdsong so you can hear it everywhere - even when you're on the BOG.

And now have our own ABSOLUTELY MASSIVE PRIVATE GARDEN - which is EPIC. Mum says we have got to be really thankful for it cos there's all these kids around us who live in tiny flats without any gardens and they are not allowed to go outside which is ACTUALLY a proper shame and I wish they could come and play with us.

And Pete was worried that they might see us from their upstairs windows out in the churchyard and feel REALLY MAD at us, but I pointed out that there were so many trees around the edge of the churchyard that we'd be well hidden.

And Dad says "just keep the NOISE down and we'll be okay."

CHAPTER 14

"Dad, hurry up!"

"Don't slam the ball like that against the church - the Rector will soon kick us out of here, backdoor or no backdoor!"

The Rector had told them that the best place for football would be the north side of the yard. Here the gravestones, instead of being upright, had been laid down flat, nestling snuggly in the grass. Peter remembered reading that the churchyard had been used as an anti-aircraft station in the war and guessed that they had been laid flat then and had remained that way.

Caleb was already doing keepy-uppies as Peter and Dad took off their coats to make a goal.

"Is it 'Goalie When'?"

"No - I don't mind staying in goal. Not as young as I used to be. Just make sure you keep the ball well away from the church windows."

Caleb and Peter ran around the churchyard in the good humour of the March sunshine, chasing, tackling and volleying shots at their father. Dad always kicked the ball right out to the far corner of the yard so the boys started to hang further away from the goal. Eventually the ball came out towards them in a long arc and both leapt up to head it. Peter, with his height advantage, reached it first and the ball ricocheted off him, landing some metres away in a patch of mean looking nettles in the shadow of the north wall of the church.

"Just getting me gloves!" Caleb yelled and ran back to his coat, which was their left goalpost. Darting over to the nettles, he started to pick his way cautiously through them like a cat on hot tiles. Peter, watching his careful stepping, suddenly spotted something.

"Hang on Cay - there's a grave under the nettles."

"Huh?" Caleb had retrieved the ball and stopped in the middle of the nettles, the football in his hands.

"Just stay there a moment - I'm going to get Dad".

"Can't we just play footy? Dad, what the heck are you doing?"

Dad and Peter came over to the nettle patch, Dad now wearing his own leather gloves and having stuffed the bottoms of his jeans into his socks.

"Can't be too careful with nettles - they're nasty little buggers. Now where did you see it, Pete?"

Peter, staying well out of the patch, pointed at Caleb. "If Cay lifts his left leg, you can see he's standing on a stone tablet."

"Coming Cay. You just keep that left leg right up, my lad!" Gingerly, Dad picked his way through.

"Have I got to hold me leg up all day? I'm not a flamingo!"

"Nearly there. Right, got you! Now let's have a look." Dad held Cay by the arms and bent over to study the ground where he was standing. Peter was right - there was a stone slab there and the nettles had been allowed to grow all over it. With his foot, Dad slowly nudged the nettles back until he could read the inscription.

NATHANIEL DAYKIN 1794

"We've found him, Pete! It's Nathaniel Daykin's grave".

In his excitement, Peter forgot about the nettles and came scrambling over to see.

"That's it - no other description. Just like William Wadsworth's grave over the fence. I'll just take a photo." He pulled his phone out of his back pocket and took several photos.

"Can I have a look?" Caleb was still standing on one leg, trying to crane his head round one hundred and eighty degrees.

"You can put your leg down now, dope. No, don't hit me!"

"Cut it out you two!" Dad hauled Caleb and the ball out of the nettle patch. "You got your photos, Pete? Now do we have a photo of William Wadsworth's grave?"

Peter scrolled through his gallery. "There you go. I got a nice shot when the Rector and archaeologist were talking. Let's go back and print them out and compare them. We can add it to the Crime Wall." Peter was already running to pick up their coats.

"Crime Wall?" Dad looked baffled.

"That's what I've set up in the kitchen - like the police do when they're investigating. They had a big wall where they stick up photos and clues to try to find links."

"I was wondering what that was all about. Glad I asked." Dad picked up his coat to follow Peter.

"But I want to play football!" Caleb was trailing behind them as they walked through the churchyard.

"Do you want us to figure out who your ghost is?"

"Yeah – but can we play football first? He won't mind. Look!"

They looked. From their bedroom window, the pale face of the watchman was staring down at them.

CHAPTER 15

"So I'm the only one who hasn't seen him?" Mum sounded distinctly disgruntled as Peter and Dad were wafting their phones at each other, ludicrously excited, comparing photos.

"Look - nothing on mine either. And we *definitely* saw him. But, look - the photo just shows the window and what you can see of the inside of the room."

"Blimey, this is all a bit, you know, spooky…" Dad murmured sheepishly.

Peter understood what he meant. It was rather unnerving to think that he could appear any minute - and the house in lockdown was crowded enough already. "Well at least Cay's not scared anymore," he pointed out.

Surprisingly Caleb had not dashed straight to his safe place under the dining table but had stayed in the kitchen as they discussed the latest appearance. "I'm not frightened of him anymore. He's okay - he knows we're trying to help him."

"Mum, can we use your printer to print these photos of the gravestones?"

"Of course - you should be able to do it by Bluetooth if it's set up right. Now I'm just making a cup of tea and then I must go back to work. Anyone else want one?"

By the end of the afternoon, the incident room (formerly known as the kitchen) was starting to take shape. Caleb had drawn some large signs which were now Blu-Tacked to the Crime Wall:

WILLIAM WADSWORTH DIED 1795

NATHANIEL DAYKIN DIED 1794

Beneath each sign was a photo of each gravestone and beneath that, an array of Post-it notes setting out all they knew about each person. Peter was drawing up a last note - "Connections" - and stuck it up between the two columns.

"So what connections have we already established. Let's have a think."

Caleb giggled. "Pete, you sound so serious!"

"Do you want to solve this mystery," Peter retorted crossly, flicking a bit of BluTack at his brother.

"Cut it out, you idiots," called Dad from the table where he was trying to fix a broken armchair. Dad had views about BluTack ending up in the wrong place and creating Work For Him To Do.

"Connections: both alive between 1780 and 1794. The archaeologist reckoned William was in his twenties when he died in 1795. Nathaniel we know was fourteen in 1794." Peter wrote this out and stuck it between the photos.

"And they both would have been around when that dodgy church warden, Merceron, was up to his tricks," Dad added.

"And they are both dead."

"Thanks Caleb".

"Well they are - I'm going to write it down." Caleb took a note and wrote 'BOTH DEAD' in capital letters.

"Does it give any more information in that book of the Rector's?"

"Nope – it just says what I've read to you. Dad, do you think I could contact that Professor bloke who wrote it? I think the Rector said she knew him."

"Good idea - why don't you call her now. The number's written on the kitchen notice board."

"But you can't contact the professor person - he'll want to know what we're doing!" Caleb looked aghast at the idea.

"I'm only asking if he's got some more information."

Caleb's face had gone very white and his freckles stood out like someone had dotted them in in brown felt-tip.

"But he's really embarrassed about something. It's us he wants to help him, not some weird freak of a professor who doesn't know him or anything!"

"But how the heck do you know that, Cay?"

"Just look - don't you have eyes!" Caleb gesticulated behind them. Peter and Dad wheeled round. There, within a metre of them, the watchman was standing, still as a tree on a calm day. Dad swore loudly and Peter felt his stomach almost jump out of his body as the watchman observed them with sad-looking eyes. With his heart pounding, Peter found himself clutching Dad. Feeling about five years old again, he buried his face in the warmth of his father's chest. The tiny part of his brain that remained unfazed by the fear tried to study the spectre. The ghost was solid but had see-through edges - like someone on a Zoom call flickering against a false background.

"Can we help you, mister?" Caleb's soft voice next to them sounded incredibly unreal.

The watchman looked at them intently. Peter was sure he could see the man's chest moving slowly in and out as the long-dead lungs tried to breathe. Was he trying to tell them something?

Brrrrrrrr! They all jumped again as Dad's phone on the table beside them vibrated violently. The ghost vanished as abruptly as he had appeared. They stared at each other, eyes wide, hardly able to comprehend what had just happened.

Dreadfully embarrassed for being so scared, Peter pulled away from his father. Dad, his face also starting to redden, gave him a self-conscious grin. Abruptly, the pantry door opened behind them, and they swung round to see Mum emerge, her hands full of the mugs she had collected in there over the course of the day.

She stared at their faces.

"Did I miss something?"

CHAPTER 16

Razzy-Razzy-Rascal, you don't have to worry any more cos the watchman knows we're trying to help him. So we don't have to HIDE here any longer to get away from him. But don't worry - this is our den so you and me can still HANG OUT here together cos it's cool.

Pete's on the phone to that PROFESSOR PERSON who wrote that history book about the church, seeing if he knows any more stuff about Nathaniel and William. Pete has promised us ABSOLUTELY that he's going to be REALLY AND COMPLETELY careful not to say anything about the ghost because the professor might think that we are all TOTALLY NUTS.

I'm so glad you're here cat cos I miss my mates big time and I haven't even got a phone to WhatsApp them. (It's not fair. Pete's got a phone but no mates - I've got loads of mates BUT NO PHONE! Which is just UNFAIR!)

Dad says we might be able to Zoom my old class next week – if there's enough Wifi for Mum to work at the same time - which I bet there won't be because she's ALWAYS on Grown up Zoom which is called 'Teams' and she never seems to do any REAL work.

Wonder how our old house is? Bet they haven't mended the roof yet but then again it was a completely HUMONGOUS tree that toppled onto it, wasn't it, SO it must have made about a BILLION pounds worth of mess.

Bet Yorkshire's really strange in lockdown. I reckon my school must be closed and that dinner lady ghost is still appearing in the empty corridors, and WONDERING where everyone is. What did she want? Do you think, Razzy, if she came here, she'd be able to ask our watchman what he wants? Do you think there's this great big place where all the ghosts come to when they're in England – a sort of motorway services where ghosts HANG OUT when they're travelling between Heaven and Earth?

I tell you something Razzy, I bet they're not doing Clap for Carers in Yorkshire. I mean, it was pretty weird last Thursday seeing all our new neighbours out on their doorstep clapping for the nurses and people who work for the NHS. But they're soft Southerners and used to doing sappy things. Can you IMAGINE Grandad and his mates clapping away like happy seals? I bet Grandad would tell that Dutch lady who suggested that we all Clap for Carers, that it's just something that YORKSHIRE PEOPLE JUST DON'T DO…

CHAPTER 17

Dad had excelled himself with tea that night though Peter suspected that it was his way of making up for being so scared by the ghost. He had created individual pots of macaroni cheese, each served straight from the oven with the cheese sauce bubbling away. The smell was delicious - a cloud of cheddar with hints of spicy nutmeg. Mum sniffed the air appreciatively.

"Tom, you've done it again. Maybe the reason your ghost is so miserable is that he can smell the food but no longer eat it. Oh come off it, Cay - you don't need ketchup with everything!"

They dug in, each craving the hot pasta as the perfect cure for their nervousness and for a while there was no sound but the chink of cutlery on ceramic. While they were eating there was a sharp knock on the front door. Dad jumped up, opened the door, yelled "thanks" at the retreating figure and came back into the kitchen carrying a bulging carrier bag.

"Here you are, Pete – delivery from Professor Blackwell. Time for you to do some research the old-fashioned way. I'm just going to wash my hands cos I've touched the bag."

Peter had just finished his meal. "Can I take the bag yet or does it need to be in quarantine with the parcels?" (Dad had set up a shelf system where parcels were moved into a safe shelf on the second day after delivery once the chance of them being infected with Covid-19 had passed.)

Dad sighed seeing Peter's eager face. "Oh go on - the files should be okay if they just been sitting the Prof's house. Try to avoid touching the actual bag and wash your hands afterwards - don't lick your fingers or anything."

Peter took his prize up to the bedroom and began reading. The mac and cheese had done its job and he started to read without fearing the presence of the ghost. Two hours later he was still at it when Mum brought him a cup of hot chocolate.

"Look at you! Proper historian aren't you, or should I say detective?"

"Same thing, I guess, when the dead body's over two hundred years old. Mum, this is totally fascinating. There's a whole bit here on Nathaniel Daykin's trial – it actually mentions the watchmen who were living here in this house!"

"Go on, hit me with it." Mum popped herself down on the other bed and started to drink her own steaming mug.

"Well – here's the deal: Nathaniel Daykin is an apprentice stonemason so he's strong and has big muscles even though he's only a teenager. One night they discover him in the churchyard stealing a body from a grave – it's the body of a woman who'd been buried there that afternoon. While the watchmen try to arrest him, he kills one of them and so they try him for murder as well as body-snatching. Here's the report of the trial. He passed the dog-eared photocopy over to her. Mum started to read it out loud:

"'Mistress Johnson had been interred on the north side of the churchyard between the yew tree and the wicket gate, which is the entrance to the yard from the Bethnal Green road.

Giving evidence, the watchman reported that he and his companion had been alert to trouble after the burial and therefore had maintained a watch on the yard from the beginning of the curfew. It had been a fine cloudless night.

After 11 of the clock, from the window of the upper room of the Watch House, he had observed someone enter the yard by means of the wicket gate and go over to the grave. He had summoned the head watchman, Samuel Weaver, who had gone out into the churchyard to investigate. A minute later, he had heard the noise of Weaver's rattle. He had run out and had found Weaver lying on the ground dead with a wound to his head. He had managed to apprehend the accused who was in the act of escaping, still carrying the spade by which Master Weaver had been bludgeoned to death.'"

"So this is the evidence which condemns Nathaniel Daykin? Pretty compelling stuff. Why was Daykin's mum so insistent her son was innocent?" Mum looked up from the photocopy, her blue eyes questioning.

"She's mentioned here," Peter pointed to a line further down the document. *'The Accused's mother interrupted the trial at this moment, calling out to the judge that her Nathaniel was a good boy and had been at home in bed on the night in question. But a witness then came forward to say that'* – now I don't quite follow the language – *'she was a professional lady who had been not at home that evening but engaged in her work with him'*. Mum - what does that mean? Was she a lawyer like you?"

Mum laughed. "Not quite - but she would have had to work long hours too, my lad! So this must have blown poor old Nathaniel's alibi?"

"Absolutely."

"But no mention of William Wadsworth?"

"None. He could have been the watchmen who gave the evidence, but they don't record his name."

Mum read the report carefully once more and looked up. "What we need to examine are the church records for that time to show who was employed by the parish."

Something jogged Peter's memory. "Hey, remember when we were moving the skeleton, the Rector said that I could come over and look at the church records if I wanted to?"

Mum sighed and put down the report. "Yes I can remember. It's a shame the church's closed for Covid - I don't think they're letting anyone in. You can call the Rector if you like but…"

Peter considered this. Like a dog who has scented a rabbit, he couldn't abandon the chase now. Another thought struck him.

"Mum, what's a wicket gate?"

"It's a small gate to let people through."

"I wonder where it was. It's all housing now between the church and the main road." Peter looked out of the window, but darkness had crept up on them and he could only just make out the outline of the church against the sky. He looked over to Caleb's bed where his mother sat still flicking through the file. As if sensing his gaze, she looked up.

"You all right Pete? It's all been a bit odd hasn't it - us coming down to London, and then lockdown – and now all this ghostly business going on."

"I'm fine. Puts off the evil day when I've got to start school down here!"

Mum came over to give him a hug. "Oh Peter - the school you've got a place at is one of the best around. You'll be fine." She stiffened abruptly. "Hey, can you hear music?"

Just then there was the sound of footsteps pounding up the stairs and Caleb burst into the room. "Pete, Mum, can you hear it?"

"The music?"

"It's coming from the church - really loud scary organ music, but the church is locked and bolted and has CHAINS across the door and EVERYTHING!!"

CHAPTER 18

There was, of course, a boring explanation to the noise coming from the church. Dad phoned the Rector and she told him that the church organist had been given official sanction to enter the church once a week to put the church organ through its paces. Apparently church organs started to fall apart if they were not played regularly.

With their window open in the warmth of the early spring evening, Peter and Caleb lay in bed listening to the music. The massive chords and delicate little fugues echoed around the churchyard until well after midnight. Mum reckoned the organist must be glad to get out of their house to play again, and what they were listening to was a very happy human being. Caleb had yawned and said he was happy for them, now could they shut up. Peter however had found it quite soothing to fall asleep to.

He was very quiet the next morning, so quiet that Dad asked him if he felt ill. (Dad, as self-appointed Head Nurse as well as Headmaster of the Home School, had bought the household a thermometer and was not afraid to use it if anyone showed any symptoms of the virus.)

"I'm fine Dad – leave me alone. I'm just mulling over the evidence."

"Mulling over the evidence? I like that." Dad was putting up some more shelves in the lounge, Caleb eagerly trying to assist him. Peter watched how his father worked, methodical, taking the greatest of care to make sure everything was measured correctly and cut neatly to size. The house was filled with the crisp smell of newly sawed wood, which Mum said was a definite improvement on the smell of damp.

"Dad - did the Rector say when the organist was next coming to play the organ?"

"She did actually," Dad called back, muffled as his mouth was holding screws, "Thursday."

Two days from now. Time to plan. But in the meantime, time to check out the wicket gate. Dad had started to drill so he had to wait until the noise ceased.

"Dad, I'm going out to the churchyard."

"Please take Cay with you. If he keeps on trying to help me, I might end up accidentally nailing him to the wall."

They wandered out into the churchyard, Caleb clutching his football. Instinctively they glanced back at their bedroom window to see if the ghost was making an appearance. But today - nothing.

"He's waiting to shock Mum big time when she's not expecting it." Peter said. Caleb nodded in agreement and then was off, dribbling the ball at speed round the graves, almost knocking over an arrangement of flowers on one of the cremation plots.

"Cay," hissed Peter, "Mum says she'll dock your pocket money if you break anything."

"Won't. I'm too good for that!" Watching his brother and the football leading a merry dance through the gravestones, the silver ball flicking here and bouncing off there like a salmon travelling up a mountain stream, Peter had to admit Caleb was right.

Leaving Caleb playing, he strode past the church entrance over to the north side to look at the wall that stretched across the perimeter, separately the churchyard from the houses beyond. It was a modern wall with regular London bricks. He turned to look at the well-shaded strip of green that comprised the north side of the churchyard and saw the nettle patch where they had found Nathaniel Daykin's grave. There was evidence of other gravestones too – all laid flat. Strange that Mistress Johnson woman would be buried here if it was the side of the yard meant for criminals, but then maybe she was a criminal too?

"Or perhaps she was just poor?" Dad suggested when he had gone back in. "The north side might have been unpopular because it's in the shade - perhaps it was cheaper to get buried there. Now will you drag Cay in for his tea please."

Peter ran out into the yard happy for the chance to talk to Caleb in private. A plan was forming in his mind, and he had realised, quite to his surprise, that for the first time in his life he needed Caleb's help.

Caleb was so quiet over tea that Peter worried that his parents would smell a large hairy rat, but Mum's head was still deep in her work and Peter put in such a good effort praising Dad's lasagne, that the unaccustomed peace went unnoticed.

The previous Thursday's inaugural Clap for Carers had seen Dad and Mum standing outside their door at eight, hesitantly clapping and looking around to see if anyone else was about. Caleb had said that it was all completely stupid and had stayed in the lounge with the television turned up. Peter himself had hidden in his room reading.

Now, as he reviewed the paraphernalia that Caleb had set up, Peter thought that whoever had dreamt up Clap for Carers might not quite have expected this. Their neighbours were in for a shock!

CHAPTER 19

On Thursday evening, the church clock struck eight. Standing on the doorstep with her freshly-polished euphonium gleaming gold in the sunset, Mum struck up with "Somewhere over the Rainbow" – the song that the Clap for Carers organisers had suggested everyone play for the occasion. Behind her, Caleb and Dad and Peter stood pounding their saucepans with wooden spoons in time to the beat. The music echoed along Forest Close in the urban canyon created by the tall buildings. As Peter struck his pan, he could see front doors opening all along the street, and people coming out onto their doorsteps to clap along with them.

By the time Mum reached the second verse, a window on the ground floor of the flats opposite had been pushed up and a piano had joined in. By the time they reached the third verse, a host of little children had appeared on a balcony two floors up and had started to sing along. Caleb gave them a huge wave with his spoon. Peter grinned. Despite feeling spectacularly embarrassed, he had to admit that Caleb's idea was working beautifully.

The music over, with instrument and pan still in hand, Mum and Dad started to call merrily to their neighbours and soon the street was abuzz with the sound of chatting. Seizing the moment, Peter and Caleb stole quietly back in the house and out through the back door. Once again, the rich sound of the organ was coming from the church. Keeping well in the shadows beneath the trees, they crept across the churchyard. "Now's our chance!"

The boys slipped in as quietly as possible through the unlocked church door. Peter recalled he had seen a crevice just inside the door - between the font and a bookshelf full of hymn books. Having 'borrowed' Dad's phone, (Dad wouldn't miss it

– he never knew where 'the blasted thing' was), he found the space and helped his brother into the hiding place, handing him the phone. "Remember," Peter whispered to his brother, "if the organist moves at all, you've got to buzz me! No getting distracted playing games." Caleb stuck his tongue out at him.

Without another word, Peter left him hiding and crept up the north aisle towards the vestry - where the Rector had indicated that the records were kept. As he passed the tomb of Sir Percival, he craned his head to see if anything of the skeleton was showing. It was indeed well hidden – he could not see any of it from the aisle.

The organ was located over where the south aisle met the chancel, where the pews ended, and the choir stalls began. The organist's back was turned towards him, so while the music played, Peter knew he was safe. By now the evening was well advanced. The reading light on the organ which illuminated the player's head had turned the rest of the church into near blackness. Peter had to feel his way along the edge of the pews to the vestry door. The door was part of a heavy carved-wood screen. He managed to locate the tiny handle which to his relief turned without a squeak and he crept in.

Once inside, with the air still ringing with music, he decided to risk the flashlight on his phone. He found a large mahogany desk with a shelf labelled *Church records*. The shelf was stacked with files, bulging with paper so that their shapes were bent out of shape. Peter sighed inwardly - this was going to take a while. Remembering Caleb sitting in the darkness on his own, he made a snap decision to take the files home to read. By removing only one or two files at a time there was far less chance of the Rector noticing and he could always sneak back in to return them.

He put his phone on the desk, its light aimed carefully at the wall, then reached up to the first file. Drawing it out, his face flushed with excitement as he realised the file was dated to the time of the watchmen and he had a sudden urge to read the file there and then. He leant forward to open the dusty cover, and then something hit him hard on his back between his shoulder blades and he yelled out in pain!

The music came to an abrupt halt.

CHAPTER 20

Peter's phone on the desk buzzed urgently as he wheeled round to face his attacker. "What the hell…"

To his utter amazement, he discovered a girl glaring at him. She was slightly taller than him, though her shadow loomed massive behind her. She held in her right hand her weapon - a red hard-backed hymnbook.

"Don't move a millimetre!" Her voice was soft and posh sounding but had an edge of steel.

Suddenly the room was ablaze with electric light. "Make sure you're standing two metres away from him, Fliss!" The commanding voice came from a silver-haired man who had appeared in the vestry to Peter's right. The organist. Peter realised that there must be another entrance to the room.

The girl promptly stepped back, still holding the book. Peter rubbed his back ruefully. The organist joined the girl. Peter figured that they must be living in the same household, so to be able to stand close to each other.

"Now you've got thirty seconds to explain yourself before I call the police."

Dragging himself back to reality, Peter gulped and wondered where to begin. Suddenly he realised how stupid it would sound - that he wanted to read the church records so that they could stop a ghost appearing. He took a deep breath. "I'm look…"

Just then the door behind him opened and Caleb rushed in. "Pete, it's turned really dark out there and you told me not to put on the light on my phone and I got really scared and then you screamed. Oh hello."

He suddenly became aware of his audience and stopped.

"There's a regular gang of you," the organist remarked but Peter noticed that the anger had gone out of his voice and he now sounded simply curious.

"There's only us two," Caleb told him. "Peter promised me I could play on his phone every day this week if I was his lookout but I got too scared because it was dark. I'm Caleb. He's Peter. We live at the Watch House."

There was a pause. The girl continued to stare angrily at them, still holding the hymnbook, but the full force that was Caleb appeared to have blown away the organist's anger.

"Well Caleb and Peter, we meet in strange circumstances. You two are most definitely not supposed to be here. I *am* supposed to be here, but on my own, so we are all somewhat in the wrong. Let's proceed on a more amicable footing." He looked sharply at the girl as he said this.

Peter found his voice. "I'm looking into some church history as a bit of a project. The Rector said I could look through the church records. I heard you playing and thought I'd take the chance to look at them while I could get into the church." He picked up his phone, which had started buzzing angrily again, and shoved it into his pocket.

The girl was watching him now with a curious look on her face. Peter studied her. She looked older than him, but not by much. She had a mass of curly brown hair and a pretty turned-up nose.

"Which school do you go to?" she asked suddenly.

"I'm supposed to be starting at St Chad's when the lockdown's over."

"Oh, I go to St Chad's. I'm in Year Nine." She said this in a slightly more friendly tone and finally lowered the book.

"Me too." Peter tried a smile.

"I'm going to start at St Wilfred's Primary," Caleb announced.

The girl ignored him and continued to watch Peter. Peter felt himself suddenly redden but then the organist spoke again.

"Well Peter and Caleb, I'm John Blackwell and this is my daughter Felicity."

"Oh, so you're the Professor!" Peter was glad to turn away from the girl's stare. "Thanks for all the papers. They were really helpful. But I needed to find out more about Merceron and the watchmen and I thought I'd see if the church records had any more information."

Professor Blackwell smiled. "Aha - the villainous Merceron. *Qui custodiet ipsos custodes* - 'who guards the guards', or I suppose you might say, 'who watches the watchmen' - as they were a bit of a bad lot back then, weren't they just! Well, there's plenty of information in there," Blackwell pointed to the shelf of files. "The earliest records are all in the first file - they date back to the time the church was consecrated, so that's probably the box you're after."

"I was going to borrow it," Peter admitted, his face beginning to blush even more, "but I promise I'll bring it back."

"Of course you will. I don't think we should all start poring over it now. But do give me a call if you want to discuss anything. I'm guessing you're interested in the watchmen because you're living in their house. Is that right?"

"Yeah, sort of." Would Cay mention the ghost? Peter was feeling beyond embarrassed already without anything else.

"It's because we found the skeleton," Caleb piped up.

"Skeleton?" Peter saw that this had got Felicity's attention. Now his ears were reddening to match his face.

"Peter says it's hiding behind Sir Percy but I'm not allowed to look because I get bad dreams."

"Seriously?" Now Professor Blackwell also seemed deeply interested. Peter explained the story of the skeleton. He led the way out of the vestry to the Knight's effigy and showed them the casket hidden behind it.

"How fascinating." Blackwell was trying to see through the plastic lid with his own flashlight. "So he was found in a marked grave but outside the churchyard. That's very interesting." There was something in Blackwell's voice that made Peter uneasy.

"We shouldn't bother him," Caleb told them. "He needs to be buried properly in the churchyard."

"How do you know that?" asked the girl.

"He doesn't," Peter told her, with a strong desire to get Caleb home before he could say anything else.

"He'll have a hard job being buried in the churchyard as it's officially full." The Professor finished examining the casket. "They'd have to get permission from the church council to fit anyone else in and that would be difficult to come by for someone who's been dead for the past two hundred years."

"But the gho…."

"Time we went home, Cay!" Peter pushed his little brother down the aisle before he could start arguing. "Thanks Mr Blackwell. I reckon I've got enough in this file to keep me busy."

"Nice to meet you, Peter and Caleb."

The girl said nothing but watched them go through lonely eyes.

CHAPTER 21

So Razzy-Razzy-Rascal, we SUDDENLY realise that it's ABSOLUTELY TERRIBLY LATE and we run out of the church and dash across the dark and probably scary churchyard. (I say probably scary because (a) we run SO FAST that I don't have time to be scared and (b) it's much MUCH more scary when we get back to the Watch House and find ourselves face to face with a MAD MUM which is just about the MOST SCARIEST thing in the whole wide world.)

(Actually, this is except for films with MAD MUMMIES in them. Which are, in FACT, dead similar to Mad Mums except that one lot are really ancient and EGYPTIAN and have bandages around their faces and go GROAN, and the other lot aren't quite as old, and get SERIOUSLY cross if you say that they ARE old, and don't have bandages, and go 'CALEB TIMOTHY ASHBY!' a lot instead of just 'groan'…)

So it turns out dear old Dad ACTUALLY NOTICED his phone was missing for the first time THIS CENTURY and went and dragged Mum from her work which is SOMETHING THAT YOU DO NOT DO IF YOU WANT TO LIVE TO TELL THE TALE.

So me and Dad sit very quietly in the corner like little mice cos there's then this HUGE AND ALMIGHTY ROW going on between Pete and Mum who is completely on the warpath and can SHOUT FOR ENGLAND when she gets going!!!!

CHAPTER 22

Peter found he had fifteen missed calls on his phone and had to account for each and every one of them. Telling the truth did not help him either.

"Why didn't you get me to call the Rector. I'm sure she would have let you in to see the records!" Mum's face was red with fury.

"But you said it wouldn't be allowed!"

"I'll tell you what's not allowed – sneaking into churches in the dead of night…"

"It was twilight."

"I'll give you twilight, Peter James Ashby! Now get up to bed this minute. You too Caleb. And I tell you something else, Peter. If your brother gets nightmares tonight about hiding in creepy churches, you're the one who's going to get up and comfort him. UNDERSTOOD?"

"Understood."

The next morning his mother's fury had lessened but was still evident, like a windy morning after a stormy night. Peter decided to secrete himself away upstairs in the bedroom to open the file he had taken from the church. It contained four black ledgers tied together with a length of red ribbon. Opening the first of the ledgers, he carried it carefully over to his desk. The pages were stained yellow with age and the writing was tiny and faded to grey, but with the aid of a magnifying glass from an old bug-finding kit of Caleb's, he found that he could just make it out.

Church Expenses the Year of our Lord 1749

Too early. He carefully leafed through the crackling pages until he found:

Church Expenses the Year of our Lord 1784

January
Church linen 1 pound, 4 shillings and 6 d.
Communion wine cask 1 shilling and 3 d

Oh man, this was going to take all day! Stifling a huge yawn, he turned onwards until he came to the mid-nineties. This was more like it. If Nathaniel's trial had been in 1794, then he should really be concentrating on the time immediately before that.

January

Church linen 17 shillings and 6d.
Communion wine cask 18 shillings and 9d.
Curate per diem (acculm.) 2 guineas and 4d.

Downstairs he heard an abrupt knocking at the door and a 'thank you!' from Caleb indicating that their online shopping was being delivered. He heard Dad open the door and start to bring in the bags. He forced himself back to the page.

Wages

To J. Corby - Sexton – 1 guinea and 1 shilling.
To S. Weaver - Watchman – 19 shillings and 6 shillings.
To W. Wadsworth – Watchman – 10 shillings and 6d.

His brain was concentrating so much on deciphering the writing that for a moment he failed to notice the significance of the last line. Then something clicked in his brain and he reread the line carefully, his finger running along each word of the ledger. He grabbed his notepad and jotted the details down and then sat back staring at the book, now feeling wide awake and rather pleased with himself.

He must have been so lost in his thoughts that it took some time for him to notice a quiet tapping. Instinctively he tried to ignore it - the house was full of the most random of noises. (Mum, the only musician among them, reckoned that the heating moaned in the key of E minor when it came on, and they all agreed that when the toilet flushed downstairs it sounded like the whole place was sneezing.) But this noise was different and it was coming from the front window. Eventually curiosity grabbed him, and he walked over to take a look. At first he saw nothing out of place. The chestnut tree was just starting to bloom and its lantern-like flowers hung heavy on its branches, so close to the window that he felt he could reach out and touch them.

Then he noticed the girl! She was sitting motionless, nestled in the crown of the tree, a few metres away from him but hidden completely from the street below. She was holding out a broken-off branch and was tapping it against his window.

With great effort (getting the windows to open at all in the Watch House was another of Dad's little triumphs) he pushed the frame up and leant out.

"Felicity?" The girl put her fingers to her lips and gesticulated that he should move back. Baffled, he did as she bid and then a paper aeroplane flew neatly past his ears and landed on Caleb's bed.

By the time he had grabbed it and come back to the window, she had gone. He looked down at the aeroplane. It was neatly folded to fly straight but Peter noticed some sort of message beneath its folded wings. He unfolded it eagerly.

The row of smiling dancing figures, each bearing a flag or

two held at different angles, made him laugh out loud as he understood. He dashed over to the bookshelf and took out his copy of "Secret Water", one of his old favourites, about some children let loose to go exploring in the islands off Suffolk. He flicked to the right page and found the semaphore alphabet laid out in the form of the dancing people. He grabbed a pencil and started to translate:

KGGGD HCACIAF

Huh? More code - an anagram? Read it backwards? He sat at his desk trying obvious ciphers such as making A equal B and so on, but nothing made sense. Anyway - what word in English had three repeated letters in the middle of it? Was it in a foreign language then?

Exasperated he lolled back on the bed. Why had she made it so complicated? Couldn't she have just sent him her phone number?

Her phone number! Of course – he had forgotten the semaphore alphabet had numbers too! He grabbed his phone, googled another version of the code and in a few seconds had reduced the dancing men to a standard eleven-digit mobile phone number. How slow he had been! All his joy at finding a kindred spirit evaporated into a cloud of embarrassment. Still there was no time to lose. He grabbed his phone and messaged her. The reply was almost instant. She must have been waiting for him.

Dad's got interested in your skeleton. Making plans to move it to the Uni where he works. Thought you would like to know. x

No, that was not the plan at all! In a sudden flash of certainty, Peter realised that Caleb was right and the skeleton needed burying in holy ground. Then he suddenly remembered his discovery in the church ledger. He rapidly texted back.

How long have we got?

No idea. Til the end of lockdown?"

Thanks. You're a star!

He definitely intended to message Felicity again, but for now that had to wait. He stuffed his phone back into his trouser pocket, grabbed the ledger and ran downstairs to share the news.

CHAPTER 23

"So this means that William *is* the ghost? It is our skelly that's haunting us?"

Caleb was jumping up and down with excitement. Dad was deep in concentration, poring over the ledger, using his finger to read the scrawling hand-writing. Even Mum had abandoned all pretence of working for the moment and was deep in debate with Peter about the consequence of the discovery.

"Well - we know that the skeleton is Wadsworth's because of the gravestone, we know the ghost is a watchman because of his clothes and his rattle, and we now know that, in life, William Wadsworth was definitely a watchman who presumably lived in this house. It's not quite definitive proof but it's good enough for me," Mum announced firmly.

Peter stuck a new label under Wadsworth's name: "GHOST". The family looked at their wall with deep satisfaction. He had another thought. "Hey, it means that William is the watchman who gives evidence at the trial! It's got to be him cos the only other watchman listed in the records for that time is Samuel Weaver who we know was murdered by Nathaniel Daykin."

"So what do we do now?" Dad asked.

"Keep going," Peter told him. "I'm going to keep going through the ledger to see if it mentions William again. But you and Cay can go through the rest of Professor Blackwell's papers to see if there's anything useful now we know who he is. I'll work in my room cos the light's better up there." *And so I don't accidentally blurt out that we've got to get this thing solved as soon as possible*, he thought to himself, figuring that girls who climb trees to send messages to you are things best kept quiet.

He left them in the kitchen leafing through the bag of papers, ran up to his room and was soon hard at work. It was so much easier now he knew he was no longer on a fool's errand. Noticing that the ledger entries were in date order, he recorded all the payments to the watchmen for 1794 and 1795. Then, seized with an idea, he read on up to the end of 1797, still recording all the wages paid to the watchmen. Finally, he went back in time to the beginning of 1793 until he had a list that covered several years.

"Grub's up!" There was a bellow from below.

"Coming!" Peter picked up his notes and ran downstairs. Dad noticed his son's keen face as he laid out ham and egg sandwiches and home-made lemonade.

"I can tell you've got some more news for us - but just hold your horses and eat your lunch. Cay and I have found something too. Your mum'll be along soon - she's just finishing a call." From behind the pantry door they could hear the muffled voices of the meeting.

Peter suddenly realised how thirsty he was. He took a great glug of lemonade. Dad had made it that morning and it was icy-cold and sharp with lemon zest.

"We've found a map of the churchyard," Caleb told him with his mouth full of ham and egg roll. "It shows the wicked gate."

"Wicket gate, Cay, and don't talk with your mouth full." It could be the effect of lockdown but Dad's tolerance of bad table manners was plummeting.

Mum arrived just then to hear Caleb's news. She took her sandwich and sat down next to Peter. Peter munched his sandwiches, happily making a mental note as to what else could be added to the Crime Wall. Suddenly he recalled something he needed to ask.

"Mum?" He approached the question carefully, not wanting to remind his mother of the previous evening. "Professor Blackwell said something about who was watching the watchmen. I didn't really understand what he was talking about."

Mum looked puzzled and then the light dawned. "Oh - was he talking about 'who guards the guards?'"

"Yeah, that was it. He said something in Latin about custodians, and then translated it as 'who watches the watchmen'."

Mum turned towards him, cup of tea in hand and a thoughtful look on her face. It was the sort of question she loved. "It's a philosophical conundrum that was first posed by a Roman poet. You give powers to the police to make sure everyone behaves, but who makes sure that the police themselves behave? Nowadays we have a Police Watchdog, which is meant to do just that, but I would imagine that Professor Blackwell's point was that it hasn't always been the case. Does that make sense? Stop giggling Caleb!"

Caleb's face was covered in mirth. "A Police Watchdog! Isn't that like an Alsatian with a great big stopwatch in its paw?"

"Nah - it'd be a Labradoodle with a Rolex," Dad chipped in. "Come on, our resident comedian, there's a dishwasher that needs a bit of love out here." Dad propelled Caleb into the kitchen.

"Cheers Mum," Peter gave his mum a quick hug. She grinned - the question had restored her humour as Peter knew it would and he finally felt forgiven.

Soon lunch was cleared away. Mum had disappeared back into the pantry and Dad, Peter and Caleb were concentrating on the plan of the churchyard. Peter could not hide his enthusiasm. "Look - this is dated 1749 - just when the church opened. And it shows all the grave plots - they're each numbered!"

"They look like car parking spaces!" This time Caleb did not seem to be put out by the notion of dead bodies 'parked' next to their house.

"Let's go and see if we can find any traces of the wicket gate."

"You and Cay can – I've got to sort the kitchen drain out." Dad sounded rather put out, as though he would far prefer to be outside with them. "No, don't take the plan - it's old and fragile. Take a photo of it – that's what phones are for."

Out of the glare of the sun by Nathaniel Daykin's grave, they studied the photo on Peter's phone.

"So." Peter traced his finger over the drawing of the church. "The church has five north-facing windows, and the gate was over here – opposite the gap between the first and second windows." They stood under the gap between the windows and surveyed the modern brick wall.

"Look!" Peter pointed to the ground. Despite the long grass, they could just make out a series of small shapes leading away from the church towards the wall. The boys ripped up bits of the vegetation and soon uncovered a row of well-worn sandstone flags set in a straight line, leading northwards and ending at the brick wall. Well satisfied by the discovery, Peter took several photos and then turned to photograph the north side of the church to put the path in its context. He paused for a moment. There was something not quite right, but he could not think what.

"It's not that exciting," pointed out Caleb. "Doesn't tell us anything new. Come on, let's play footy - you promised me!"

Peter gave up and ran to join his brother.

After Dad had got the drain gurgling again and Mum had popped out to the kitchen for a cup of tea, Peter showed them his photo of the path to the wicket gate, now printed out and stuck to the kitchen wall. Mum sipped her drink while studying the plan spread out in front of her on the table.

Dad had a thought. "What were you going to tell us when you came down for lunch, Pete?"

"Oh yeah - the watchmen's wages. I'll just grab my notebook." He dashed upstairs, grabbed it and ran down again. "Now it hasn't quite got the wow factor of Cay's map," he told them quickly, "but it is a bit odd. This ledger records how much each watchman was paid by the church at the end of each month. I went back as far as January 1793 – at this point there's only the one watchman, an "S. Weaver", who must be the Samuel Weaver who was murdered by Nathaniel Daykin – we know that from the record of the trial."

"Now - Weaver gets paid 19 shillings every month. In September 1793 William Wadsworth joins him. He gets 10 shillings and 6d a month - 'd' means old pence I think?"

Mum nodded. "Go on Pete. Caleb, stop making those stupid yawns."

"But I don't understand all this weird stuff! And what's a shilling?"

"Old money, Cay. Twenty shillings equalled a pound, and twelve pennies made a shilling. Oh and twenty-one shillings made a guinea."

"But what's a guinea?"

"Twenty-one shillings…"

"Aaahhh!" Caleb made to bang his head on the table.

Mum relented. "It's old-fashioned money, Cay. They were used before the pound was invented but I think they still use guineas for buying and selling horses even today."

"How do you know all this?" Peter asked Mum, impressed.

"Because I've got a mind that sucks up all sorts of random facts. Now go on."

"Well, after June 1794 two things happen - Samuel Weaver's name stops appearing then which must mean he's now dead. But - here's the interesting thing: William Wadsworth gets an absolutely <u>massive</u> increase in salary – he's now paid 2 guineas every month!"

"Go on." At least his parents looked keen. Behind their backs, where only Peter could see, Caleb was miming loading a shotgun and shooting his foot. Peter ignored him and pressed on.

"In August 1794 there's a new watchman named Matthew Hartley but Hartley's only paid the lower rate of 10 shillings and 6d. In January 1795 William's name disappears – must be when he dies, and after that only Hartley's name appears in the ledger, still being paid the lower rate." He finished with a deep breath.

"So the killer question is why our William is being paid so much more than the others." Dad started to tap the table with his thumb. This was something he always did when he was thinking.

Peter nodded. "I've checked the payments for the two years before and two years after, and although there are other watchmen listed, no one gets nearly as much money as William Wadsworth."

Mum had a thought. "Perhaps it was danger money - you know, after Samuel Weaver is killed, they have to pay William more to stay on his own?"

Dad shook his head. "I'm not sure. It's a heck of a lot of money and surely they would then have cut his wages again once the new bloke starts, but they don't."

They sat there quietly, thinking round this new issue while Peter wrote the question on a piece of paper and stuck it to the Crime Wall. He took a black marker pen and drew and arrow and stuck that between the question and William Wadworth's name. Just then the sun went in and the kitchen quickly grew dark as though rain was about to come.

Suddenly there was a howl from the other end of the table. Rascal the cat who had been sitting in his basket snoozing, leapt up thoroughly startled. Knocking over his chair in a desperate bid to escape, Caleb fled from the room!

CHAPTER 24

Peter and his parents exchanged glances.

"I'll go." Dad said wearily. He walked quickly into the lounge where Caleb was crawling under the dining table. Dad leant down and peered at him through the chair legs.

"Come on Cay, what's up now?"

"It's the ghost! He's REALLY cross with us!"

"How do you know that?"

"Just LOOK!" Caleb screamed and pointed behind Dad's shoulder. Dad wheeled around.

Standing about a metre away in the doorway through which he had just walked, was the watchman. The lounge was much brighter that the kitchen but despite the light, Dad felt like he'd walked under a dark rain cloud and found himself shivering uncontrollably. The watchman's face was a picture of fury, the young face twisted and contorted with bitter anger!

There was absolute silence. The room seemed to be filled with a desperate rage as though they were being silently yelled at. It was a horrible feeling. Dad backed so far away from the door that he crashed into the dining table; Caleb cowered under it, his hands over his ears and his eyes tight shut.

Then there was a most almighty noise! Rascal had arrived at the door to the room and was hissing and spitting and yowling at the spectre, his fur standing on end making him look like a demented ginger loo-brush.

The ghost vanished. Rascal remained on guard. He was oddly watchful, his nose sniffing here and there as if waiting for a mouse, his fur still raised up.

"Oh my…" Dad found he could move again although his heart was beating fit to burst. He wiped his sweaty palms on his trousers and then bent down to help Caleb out. Caleb still had his eyes tightly shut. Peter and Mum arrived in the doorway, looking curiously at the feline fury in front of them.

"What just happened?" Mum asked, mystified.

"Tell you in a minute. Can you put the kettle on, love? I <u>really</u> need another cup of tea."

Soon the family were sitting in the kitchen drinking tea like there was no tomorrow and working their way through a packet of chocolate Hobnobs. The candle that Caleb had been given by the Rector blazed away in the centre of the table.

"Are you sure you want to see the ghost now, Mum?" Peter asked teasingly. Mum gave him a look over the top of her mug.

Dad was tapping his thumb on the table as if trying to tap out Morse code and then turned in bewilderment to Caleb. "But why is he so mad with us all of a sudden? Didn't you say that he was pleased with us for investigating why he's not buried in the churchyard?"

"He was happy with us, I felt it. But something's upset him."

They fell silent for a moment and watched the candle shining in the gloom.

Peter sighed. "We can't even ask the Rector to come and say another prayer because of lockdown. Hey," he gave a wild giggle, "perhaps she can do an exorcism by Zoom?"

"Yeah you can imagine it – "if there's anybody there, please press the thumbs up icon!"" Dad gave a nervous laugh.

"Shush, you two. I'm trying to think!" Mum had turned away from the table and was staring intently at their Crime Wall. Caleb, with Rascal in his arms, nestled up to her. She stretched out her arm around him protectively while continuing to look at the photos. "Now here's a thought. Remember in March when the storm blew that massive tree onto our roof? And we were all cross and upset. Who was the most angry?"

No one said anything. They were busy remembering the crash of the roof and the confusion and the real fear that their whole house was going to come down on top of them.

"Well I'll tell you. It was me. I was absolutely livid. And do you know why? It was because it was my fault the tree came down. I was supposed to be organising a tree surgeon to come round all last summer and I never did, so when the storm brought the blasted thing down, causing us to be scared out of our wits and leaving us homeless, well there you go. I was so ashamed of myself and that shame showed itself disguised as anger."

The candle continued to burn vividly in the centre of the table.

"So you think William is angry now because he's done something wrong and he feels terrible about it?" Peter looked thoughtful.

"It's a good bet isn't it? There's got to be a good reason why he was buried outside the churchyard."

"And we're about to discover it." Dad looked longingly at the bottle of whisky on the sideboard. "I tell you something, I'm not sure I want to be around to see his face when we do find out."

Caleb whimpered and snuggled up closer to Mum.

Peter finished his third biscuit and looked up at them. "So we have a choice. Do we carry on investigating in the hopes that eventually we'll find out enough information to let William be buried properly. Or do we abandon the task and live out lockdown in the presence of an increasingly-spooked spook?"

Dad and Caleb moaned. "S'all right for you Pete, you didn't see him this afternoon."

"Well I'm going to carry on anyway." Peter told them. "To be honest, we're so close that we can't give up now."

His phone buzzed on the table. Crap. It might be Felicity - and there was no way he wanted his family to see! He grabbed it and stuffed it in his jeans pocket, hoping his face would not give him away.

Mum smiled at him. "That's the spirit, Peter. Oh - if that's Granny, can you tell her I'll call her later."

Peter gathered together the ledger and papers. "I'm going to go back upstairs to keep looking through the church records. See if there are any other clues."

"Stay down here with us, Peter. Surely you want the company." Dad sounded like he was pleading.

(Oh bother. This was going to be complicated.)

"I'm all right - I need the space to think sometimes." A crazy ghost of a watchman, however mad, was definitely preferable than having his whole family find out about Felicity. He carried the papers upstairs to the bedroom, sat down on his bed and checked WhatsApp.

Dad is on a mission to steal the skeleton. He is going to grab it next week on Tuesday when he goes in to play the organ. F xx

Peter cherished the two kisses. They made him feel about two feet taller. He messaged her back quickly:

You have probably worked it out, but it's a bit important to my family that the skeleton gets buried in the churchyard. Can we stop your dad getting into the church?

Even better - I've got the church key. Meet you there tonight at 11 to hide the skeleton.

Peter lay back on his bed and stared out of the window at the sky. His heart started to race with excitement and he told himself to ignore his dread of breaking rules. Just think about it, he reasoned, you're just going out of the house into your garden, going into a building, hiding the skeleton and coming home. It's absolutely no big deal. Mum and Dad will never know.

And, he reasoned further, it's for our own good as we all need the ghost to rest in peace.

The ghost! Peter sat up with a flutter of fear - what if it

appeared in his bedroom? But the day had turned into a glorious spring evening and the low sun was now shining intensely through the window. This made it harder to be scared of a wandering spirit, even one with anger issues. He went back to staring out of the window, thinking about Felicity's plan. He would need to be prepared - he would have to do something about the back door as it creaked like crazy. Perhaps he should put some margarine on the hinges before he went to bed?

As he was thinking, he surveyed the view. It was a fine sight. The side of the church facing him was bathed in a ruddy-gold glow. The trees, now rich with blossom, were standing around, motionless in the calm.

Then Peter jumped up, ran over to his desk and rifled frantically through his papers until he found the report of Nathaniel Daykin's trial. He started at the testimony of William Wadsworth.

"After 11 of the clock, from the window of the upper room of the Watch House, he had observed someone enter the yard by means of the wicket gate and go over to the grave."

But it would have been impossible to see the wicket gate from the upper room of the Watch House.

William had lied!

CHAPTER 25

Peter took a deep breath and told himself to stay calm. He must check out everything before rushing to conclusions.

First, he ran into his parents' bedroom to check the view from the window there. But it was the same. There was simply no way that a watchman looking out from the Watch House could have seen anyone enter the churchyard through the wicket gate, and then go over to a grave on the north side of the church. The church was completely in the way.

Could the church have been extended since that time? He remembered the architect's plan they'd found in Blackwell's papers so he hurried down the stairs, leaping the last three steps to save time.

"Peter!" Dad and Caleb looked up in astonishment as he shot into the kitchen.

"The plan! The plan of the church when it was first built. Where is it?"

"Here on the shelf where we've been keeping all the important documents."

"Can you clear the table - I need to spread it out."

Sensing the urgency in his son's voice, Dad left off making their tea and did what he was told, rapidly removing mugs and plates and clearing off the crumbs. Caleb carefully lifted the Rector's candle and placed it high on a shelf where it could continue to watch over them.

Peter spread out the plan. The current church building was exactly the same as it always had been. No sudden extensions out of the front. No great roof elevations to raise the ridge of the roof above what had always been intended.

"I know why the ghost is so angry."

With Caleb and Dad hanging onto every word, Peter explained his latest finding. Then he had to explain everything again as Mum came out of her pantry, her ears pricked, curiosity getting the better of her.

"So William the Watchman is paid big money to lie at Nathanial's trial and, crucially, it's due to these lies that Nathaniel Daykin, aged just fourteen, is convicted of murder and sentenced to hang!"

They fell silent.

The sun had now set and they had not noticed how dark it had become. Peter realised that it was only the flickering light from the candle that was allowing him to still make out the photos on the Crime Wall.

Suddenly there was a crash from the stairs. Mum jumped, Dad yelled and Caleb, letting out a scream that would of itself put terror into the hearts of all who heard it, dived under the kitchen table and whimpered for the cat.

"Oh crap!" Peter's heart started pounding in his chest once more.

Mum marched through the door to the stairs and switched on the light. Peter hurried after her. On a shelf at the top of the stairs, a large blue vase of flowers had stood. Now the vase lay strewn in pieces at various intervals over the steps with the flowers scattered in pools of dripping water. "I always said it was a daft place to put a vase. Anyone of us could catch it going past." Mum grinned ruefully at Peter, her voice shaky. He smiled back and took her hand, his heart still racing away like a crazy drum solo.

Mum swiftly pulled herself together. "Now Pete, would you be an angel and pop and get the dustpan?" Peter went back into the kitchen. Dad had crawled under the table and was trying to persuade Caleb to come out - Peter reckoned that Dad would be quite happy to stay under there with him. He switched on the kitchen light - a fierce but effective fluorescent tube and the room was filled with brilliant light. Dad crawled out looking rather bashful.

"Nice one Pete. I'll get on with tea."

Peter went back out to the stairs to give the dustpan to Mum and then paraded around the house switching on every light in every room.

"It's like the Blackpool illuminations in here!" Dad remarked but Peter noted the relief in his voice. Caleb emerged warily from under the table.

At that point Peter's phone buzzed. No – he could not look at it now, not in front of everyone. Usually, only Granny messaged him and never more than once a day. He pushed past Caleb and went to the bathroom and locked the door.

You up for it? F xx

Course he was up for it.

Yep. See you at 11 at the church porch.

Narthex.

Narthex then. Whatever.

At teatime the atmosphere was tense. No one wanted to discuss the watchman. Peter saw how his parents and brother seemed to be avoiding looking at the Crime Wall or the documents piled up on the side table.

"How's Granny?" Mum asked between mouthfuls of shepherd's pie.

"Wha?" Peter hastily swallowed his mashed potato. "Oh - yeah, she's fine."

"She's messaging you loads today." Caleb piped up with a flash of knowledge in his dark eyes. "She even messaged you just now."

"Grandad's lost his phone and she was telling me about them searching for it." Peter replied, extemporising wildly and hoping his face wouldn't go red.

"Bit weird though isn't it. She'll be listening to the Archers at this time - she always does."

"So."

"Just saying."

Luckily Dad changed the subject. "I was wondering whether we should all sleep in our bedroom tonight. Just for the company - we could bring in the mattresses from your beds. You could stay up late Cay and go to bed at the same time as Pete so you're not on your own."

Caleb visibly relaxed. "Yeah - I'd like that Dad."

"I mean, we can't all fit under this table." Dad tried a weak joke.

Peter tried to keep his face straight and not show the horror he felt at this suggestion. "I'm okay in my own bed, really I am."

"But Peter - I think we'd sleep better knowing that we're all together." Clearly even Mum was feeling it.

Peter was not going to give in. "But I like my privacy. It's bad enough having to share with Cay, and I snore - really badly. Must be the pollution down here."

Caleb began to cry and Mum became cross. "Peter James Ashby, will you just stop thinking of yourself for once! All we're asking is that for one night, for one flipping single night, you shift your mattress into our room so we can stay together and be safe against this…this… evil spirit that's wandering this house. Now is that too much to ask?"

Caleb continued to cry - big tears pouring down his face. Pushing her dinner aside, Mum took her younger son into her arms.

"He's not an evil spirit!" The realisation hit Peter like an express train and he stood up quickly, his chair clattering backwards. "He's desperate and lonely and feels incredibly guilty. He's been forced to do something terrible and has had to live with that for over two hundred years!"

Mum looked as though she was going to say something but then felt better of it. Peter carried on, now absolutely certain in his mind. "He's angry now as you said - because we've found out that he lied and took money for it - and he's totally and utterly ashamed of that. But he won't hurt us. I bet knocking that vase over took loads of effort. And he knows that really WE'RE ON HIS SIDE!"

There was silence.

A gust of air burst through the room as though someone had opened a window on a windy day. The Rector's candle, high on its pedestal flickered vividly but stayed alight. Then, as quickly as it came, the breeze went.

They looked at each other. Caleb stopped crying.

"Does anyone feel…calmer?" Dad asked tentatively.

"I reckon he heard us," Peter remarked with satisfaction in his voice.

CHAPTER 26

So, to Peter's great relief, they decided to go to bed in their own bedrooms. Caleb went first accompanied by the Rector's candle, and then Peter and Dad played Super Mario Kart till the clock showed ten thirty. Mum, who had been yawning since tea and was finding it hard to keep awake while still responding to emails on her work phone, murmured good night and went upstairs. Dad looked up at the clock and yawned too.

"Weird isn't it, not having anything to have to go to bed for. Normally..." (By this he meant in their pre-lockdown life up in Yorkshire when he had a job and Peter had school) "I'd been in bed by now cos I'd need to get up at 6.30 to go to the yard. And you'd need to get up to catch the school bus."

He got up off the sofa and started to put things away. Peter jumped up to help him.

"Leave it Dad - I'll stack the dishwasher and lock up. You go up."

Dad looked tired and there were lines around his eyes that Peter had not noticed before. He looked at his son gratefully.

"Okay. Night Pete. Look out for that watchman of ours!"

Peter took the glasses and mugs into the kitchen and slowly put them in the dishwasher, making sure the work was still in progress when his father came out of the bathroom and back through the kitchen. Then, after hearing him go upstairs and the floorboards creaking, he put on his old Crocs and a dark blue hoodie. He tiptoed over to the fridge, took out the Flora and removed the top layer with a sheet of kitchen roll. With the roll in one hand, he opened the back door with the other as quietly as he could and then smeared the hinges with the margarine. He glanced at the clock above the Crime Wall - ten fifty. Good.

He swapped into his school shoes, walked noisily out of the kitchen to the stairs and climbed halfway upstairs. Then he walked backwards downwards, emphasising the tread slightly to give the impression he was getting nearer to the listeners rather than further away. Once at the bottom again he stepped lightly into the kitchen, swapped back into his Crocs and slipped out of the back door.

Pocketing the key, he pulled his hood up around his face and walked swiftly across the churchyard to the main door. The moon was full and the churchyard was filled with its purple glow. Peter slipped in and out of the trees as he darted across. He glanced back at the Watch House but there was no one stirring.

A police siren sounded in the distance and Peter quickened his pace, realising that what he was about to do was now strictly against the law, even if they did have the key.

He turned around the corner to face the front entrance to the church. It was an elevated entrance – five wide steps led up to the door, with a discrete concrete ramp concealed behind them and all spot-lit by the moon. He backed off and skulked under a nearby plane tree in the shadows. And waited.

The church clock struck eleven, its sonorous voice making him jump. He stepped back, his cheeks burning. To be frightened by a church clock in a churchyard!

And then someone did grab him! Hands clasped round his mouth muffling his startled yell. He kicked his legs behind and was pleased to make contact. The hands released him.

"What the…! Felicity!"

The girl was bent over rubbing her leg. "Good reaction, Peter - you got me right in the knee."

"And you gave me a blooming heart attack!"

"Shhh! If it had been the Poliss, you'd have given them something to think about!"

"All I can say is that I'm glad you're on my side and not against me. We *are* on the same side?"

"Course we are, Didiot! Come on. Let's get skelly-shifting!"

Rather reluctantly, Peter left the safety of the shadows and followed her quickly across the path up to the church door. Feeling like he could be seen by anyone for miles around, Peter waited anxiously while Felicity produced a formidable set of keys. She selected the largest key he had ever seen, fitted it to the door and with a murmur of effort, opened the deadlock. Then she fished out a much smaller key and unlocked the yale. She opened the door a fraction and then stopped.

"You stay here a sec. I'm just going to switch off the alarm."

This was achieved in an instance and soon Peter found himself standing inside the church.

"That was pretty quick."

"Oh I always do it for Dad. He's a complete scatterbrain and has no idea what goes on. He's always thinking about his work and his research and his oh-so-important department. Which is absolutely fine if I didn't have to be with him twenty-four seven cos of this ridiculous lockdown!"

"Oh crap - shouldn't we be standing two metres apart?" Peter stepped away from her.

"Yeah and haven't I just hugged you in the churchyard?"

Peter hadn't thought of that. He remembered the closeness of her body - now he was able to think about it without being scared out of his wits.

"Anyway - are we going to move your skeleton or not?"

"Oh yeah, sure." Peter found himself fumbling for words and missing. He reached for his phone and activated the flashlight. The church was flooded with moonlight but the sharp artificial light lit up the nooks and crannies that might serve as a hiding place.

"Hey, be careful with that!"

"Huh?"

"If anyone sees it from outside, they'll think the church is being burgled. We can manage by the moonlight, I reckon."

Feeling yet again like a proper fool, Peter switched the light off. "So why does your dad want to steal the skeleton?" he asked as they strolled cautiously up through the church.

"Like I said - he wants it for his stupid history department. He's always after interesting things from the past that have a story about them. Like a grave that's dug deliberately outside the churchyard – it's just the sort of thing he's into. Now where are we going to hide it?"

They stopped by the tomb of Sir Percival. In the moonlight it loomed even bigger than it actually was - a relic of medieval times looking rather out of place. It was made up of a rectangular sarcophagus that reached up to Peter's waist. On top, attached to the lid of the tomb, lay the effigy - a crusader knight depicted in dark wood, laid out as if asleep, with the offending cat lying under his feet. An arch supported by two great pillars at his head and foot rose above the tomb, supporting a stone canopy.

Peter had a thought. "I don't suppose this is loose?" He was looking at the lid of the sarcophagus.

"Could be." Felicity cottoned on straight away. They took the rim of the lid and tried to prize it open and to their delight it started to move. It was clearly made of something much lighter than stone.

"Hang on," Peter had another thought. "What if his bones are in here?" He nodded to the effigy.

"So what if they are? We'll get him to budge up!"

"Hmm." Peter was not particularly comforted by this thought, but Felicity was enthusiastically manhandling the lid off the top of the base. Peter grabbed the other end before it fell and together they rested it on the floor. The effigy looked even more odd laid down on the tiles.

"If anyone sees him, they'll think a homeless person has crept in to go to sleep," Felicity giggled.

Peter switched his flashlight back on and was investigating the inside of the tomb. "Nowt there." He tried to keep the sound of relief out of his voice.

"Nowt there!" echoed Felicity, mocking his accent.

"Shut up!"

"Shoot up!"

Peter shone his light into her face, and, while she was blinded, tickled her under her arms. She shrieked with laughter and immediately retaliated. He dropped his phone to defend himself and for several minutes they gasped and giggled in the dark. Until they stopped, finding their arms around each other and perilously close…

Peter suddenly found himself kissing Felicity. Her warm lips touched his own and he felt a bolt of excitement rush through him. He gasped and for a moment the world stopped spinning.

"Hey, you're not a bad kisser." Felicity stroked the back of his head as they eventually moved apart.

"You're not so bad yourself!" He grinned and moved to kiss her again, but she shook her head and gently pressed her index finger to his mouth.

"Later, my lovely. Anyway, we can't stay here all night. Let's get your skelly safely hidden."

They got to work and gently lifted the casket into the base of the tomb. It was a perfect fit and they lowered it gently to the bottom. Then they raised the lid off the floor and placed it back onto the top of the sarcophagus. With the wooden knight now reclining over him, the remains of William Wadsworth were safe. Peter shone his flashlight around to make sure nothing was amiss.

"We'd better get back." Felicity took him by the hand and they walked out of church. Peter waited outside the door while she set the alarm and locked up.

"Good night's work, hey?" She pulled him close to her and gave him another kiss. Peter had a sudden crazy desire for the moment to go on for ever.

But then, without another word she was off. Peter watched her go until she was swallowed up by the shadows. Feeling like he wanted to burst into song (but remembering that this would be a stupid thing to do in the circumstances) he wandered in a happy daze back to the Watch House, with just enough clarity in his mind to open the back door extremely quietly and tiptoe softly to bed.

CHAPTER 27

So Razzy-Razzy-Rascal - I am drawing up A PETITION to allow me to camp in the back yard - not the churchyard of course cos that would be WAY TOO SCARY with all them graves, but the tiny back yard that Dad has filled with flower pots and tomato plants and his bike (which he is supposed to be going off on for bike rides for EXERCISE but seems to have completely forgotten about).

My new Akela (who is supposed to be CHIEF WOLF but is actually a lady called Julie with a BRIGHT PINK face who's in charge of Zoom Cubs) says we need to camp out in OUR GARDENS next Friday night cos it's a LOCKDOWN CAMP. No, I hadn't heard of one of them before now, either so don't look at me with your big green eyes like I'm thick.

Mum says the only way I can camp out is if Peter camps out with me cos this is LONDON NOT YORKSHIRE and anyway I'll get FREAKED OUT in the middle of the night and will probably WAKE UP the whole of Bethnal Green.

And Peter says he would prefer to STICK PINS IN HIS EYES and that everyone knows he HATES camping.

And Mum told him to grow up and he went off in a SUPER SUPERCILIOUS SULK. So Mum says I can camp in the lounge instead, but I don't want to camp inside because, well because it's haunted - OBVIOUSLY!

So I need you to sign my petition - you just need to dip your paw in this paint and… no, don't run off over the carpet, you're leaving BLUE MARKS everywhere and Dad'll kill me!

Oh crap! Come back, you stupid moggy!

CHAPTER 28

Mum's work continued from deep within the pantry. Despite lockdown, the corporate world still wanted money to buy more things and still needed lawyers to write the agreements.

Dad was now embracing his new life and was filling his time between his garden (the tiny back yard garden was abundant with grow-bags and planters) and arguing on the phone with the supermarket at its never-ending ability to mess up their online order with substitutions.

In his bedroom Peter was trying to concentrate on their work but it was not easy as he had reached a brick wall in the evidence, and his mind was elsewhere. He paused, staring blankly out of the window, listening to Dad on the phone.

"I'm telling you - this week's delivery is nothing like what I ordered. I mean - Chelsea Buns for bread rolls? And why the heck have you sent me a Black Forest Gateau? What's that supposed to be?"

With a watchful eye on his own phone and on the tree outside his window (there had been absolutely zero communication from Felicity since the night of their adventure), Peter tried to concentrate on the investigation and think where to look next.

"Yorkshire puddings! The gateau's supposed to be a substitution for the Yorkshire puddings we ordered? Am I actually hearing this right?"

He had now read through all the church records and the file given to him by Professor Blackwell and had taken to playing football with Caleb, or walking the streets with Dad in the hope that in doing something different, inspiration might come.

And indeed it did - that evening from a most unlikely source.

Dad had wanted to watch a Netflix film about the notorious Kray twins and their crimes. Peter was lurking in his bedroom, not because he had anything against a film about the Krays, but because he wanted to avoid the inevitable protests from Caleb about why they did not have more than one television and that Dad was a Complete Dictator In Imposing His Stupid Programmes On Them.

He listened as the argument ran its course. Eventually he heard feet marching upstairs and the door to his bedroom was flung open as an angry Mum propelled a howling Caleb into the room.

"And you do not say one more word but put your pyjamas on and clean your teeth. No, I don't care if the ghost comes to get you. If he's any sense he's well out of here haunting somewhere more peaceful! Sorry Pete."

"S'all right." This was Peter's cue to go and join Dad. But as he was making his way downstairs, his father's face appeared at the lounge door.

"Pete - the film – it's talking about Merceron!"

Peter dashed down the last few steps and flung himself onto the sofa. The film, which was actually a history of criminal gangs of London, was starting with the blunderbuss-ridden world of eighteenth-century London when corrupt officials such as Joseph Merceron held sway.

To their delight there was a shot of the Watch House as the film showed how the Reverend King had discovered church warden Merceron's underhand behaviour, eventually uncovering a sordid tale of corruption. It described how Merceron had made his money in the brickyards - the East End being full of brick yards at that time to supply the expansion of fashionable London.

As Merceron had a man in every yard, and knowing that a disruption at one yard could quickly threaten another, the owners would pay Merceron handsomely to ensure their work could continue. With this money he was able to buy up property and make a handy profit exploiting tenants. If they complained to the courts their petitions fell on deaf ears as Merceron, by either threatening or bribing the officials, contrived to control the whole district.

Dad was leaning forward so not to miss a word. Peter was frantically scribbling all the information down. Even Caleb sidled back into the room in his pyjamas, pretending not to be interested at all but nonetheless alert to everything.

The film explained that although the Reverend King did expose Merceron, as soon as the good priest left the parish, the villain bounced back. It was only after 1815 that his activities seemed to finally have ceased. There were rumours that a merchant arrived back in town with a score to settle against Merceron so, the film concluded, forcing Merceron to lie low and retire.

As the film turned to more modern subjects, Dad switched the TV off.

"Did you get all that?"

"Yep. What a complete git!"

"No wonder they didn't listen to poor old Nathaniel's mum when she told them he was innocent." Mum had come back into the room. "Oh you've switched it off! I was wanting to watch the rest of it."

"Oh sorry." Dad obligingly switched it back on and they were soon immersed in the Swinging Sixties and the allure of the Kray Twins' underworld.

Peter lay in his bed that night. He was finding it hard to sleep as the room was too hot and was bathed in the glow of the Rector's candle - Caleb being unable to go to sleep without it. As the shadows danced on the walls, Peter realised he was feeling properly miserable – the dark glamour of the Krays' criminal activities in the very streets where he lived, was unsettling. But it was seeing all those people milling around in the shops and streets that made him realise how much he was missing normal life.

Even Jake Webb? No. He was still happy to be miles and miles away from that stupid moron. But there were some people at his old school that he had thought of as friends, and he was painfully aware of the lack of messages from them, as though he had been forgotten straight away, like a harmless supply teacher who takes an uneventful lesson and who quickly fades from the collective memory.

And now Felicity.

Maybe there was something wrong with his phone. Maybe it simply was not picking up messages because of an issue with the Wifi? He had to admit it was unlikely. Granny was sending him messages daily.

But had something happened to Felicity? From what she had told him, things were miserable at home - perhaps her dad had found out and had become really angry with her and locked her up or something?

It suddenly dawned on him that in twenty-four hours' time, Blackwell was intending to steal the skeleton. If the professor had locked Felicity in her own house, it would be left to him, Peter, to rescue her. What were his chances of sneaking out again and hiding in the church - this time without his brother to give him away - to steal the professor's keys while the man was looking for the skeleton?

But then suddenly a wash of anger swept over him. It was more likely she simply didn't care about him and he was just some silly 'didiot' whom she'd come across and wanted to have some fun with.

As the candle burned down, his thoughts grew darker. What was the point of this whole stupid project anyway? Who could tell whether the ghost was really the watchman or just a shadow of the past with absolutely no connection with the grave next door? The house was rumoured to have been haunted for years – the Rector had said so. Could he really be bothered anymore with it? They were going to move out of the Watch House as soon as Covid was over, Mum had said. The next inhabitants could deal with the blasted thing and good luck to them!

He turned his pillow over to see if its coolness would soothe him, but to no avail. As the night wore on he lay awake, too miserable to succumb to sleep and too depressed even to read. Sleep only came when the first lines of light seeped in under the bedroom curtains.

CHAPTER 29

Peter woke in the morning with a headache to find fur tickling his nose. Rascal had abandoned his usual resting place (between Caleb's feet) and had crept onto his own pillow. He tickled him behind the ear and the cat purred sweetly.

That's someone easy to please, he thought grudgingly. He checked his phone (nothing), slipped out of bed and went downstairs to where Mum was trying to open a box of Yorkshire Tea. She was peering at the box just a little too closely. Peter watched her for a minute until he finally took pity on her.

"Do you want me to get your glasses?"

"Oh would you, love. I think they're in the bathroom. I can't see a ruddy thing on this box."

He obliged and she put the glasses on, finding the golden thread and within minutes was savouring her first brew of the day. Now caffeined up, she looked up at him gratefully, and then frowned.

"What's up Pete?"

"Nothing."

"You sure? You've got a face like a rainy weekend in Bridlington."

Peter tried to rearrange his features into something he could pass off as a smile to put her off the scent.

"Oh come on you daft ha'p'orth." Mum got up and pulled her chair up to his so she could put her arm around him. "It's all getting to you, isn't it? This Covid rubbish, this not being able to go to school and things. We're really landed at the wrong time down here haven't we? And it's really been tough on you two."

To his horror, Peter realised that a tear was rolling down his cheek. He hastily brushed it away. Mum held him close.

"And you're doing brilliantly with this… this research." She gesticulated at the Crime Wall. "You've uncovered so much about William. No one's seen him for days now - I really think you've given him a sense of peace."

Peter shrugged her off, annoyed. "But that's it, Mum. We haven't got to the bottom of it. The skelly's still in the church and the very best result is that he'll be carted off to some cemetery outside London. The ghost's still around to spook us and I've no more ideas."

"Well don't you worry about that. We haven't had a family conference about it for a while, have we? Let's have one tonight after I've finished work and we can go through all the evidence once more. Does that sound like a plan?"

He nodded, embarrassed but pleased that she had noticed. There was a click from the letterbox in the hallway.

"Too early for the post. Must be just a flyer or something. Can you stick it in the recycling please – and don't forget to wash your hands afterwards."

"Yes Mum." He replied in his most robotic voice reserved for when Mum treated him as though he were five years old. But Mum's mind was now back on her work and she failed to notice.

He strode into the hallway and found the paper that had been shoved through the letter box. It was indeed a flyer – it seemed to be window cleaners offering their services. Weird – there was no phone number or email address or indeed any way to contact them. He turned it over but the other side was blank.

His heart suddenly missed a beat as he read the copy properly.

"Want your windows cleaned?

We are the best in town."

(A rough sketch of a bucket of water and a ladder.)

Then:

"For Pete's sake, give us a go!"

There was the faintest smell of lemon.

He knew just what to do but he must do it quickly before Dad or Caleb came downstairs. He darted into the kitchen, and, after checking that Mum was safely installed in her pantry, grabbed the iron from the cupboard, switched it on and started to iron the blank side of the paper carefully.

As he had suspected, faint brown wording started to appear as the invisible lemon juice heated up. He continued until he had heated the entire paper then switched the iron off and sat down at the table, the cereal boxes hiding the paper from view.

The message was short and to the point.

"Peter. I've lost my phone. Dad is going to steal the skeleton tonight. Meet you churchyard at 8. F xxxx"

Peter felt a sense of pure joy. So she hadn't forgotten him - he wanted to run out onto the streets and start dancing! He now viewed the day ahead with a renewed sense of purpose. He would go back through *everything* they knew about William and Merceron and Nathaniel Daykin. He would get to the bottom of it all. And the first thing to do was to get Dad and Caleb to help him!

Just over an hour later Mum materialised from the pantry to find Peter holding forth to a bleary Dad and a just-about-awake Caleb. He had the red marker pen in his hand. "Remember the questions we asked at the beginning when we set up the investigation?" He indicated the large white piece of paper he had stuck onto the kitchen wall and started to scribble madly.

INVESTIGATON

Who was William Wadsworth?

Answer - a watchman.

William's boss = the senior watchman Samuel Weaver.

SW was murdered in June 1794 and William was watchman on his own until August 1794 when Matthew Hartley joined him.

In January 1795 W stops being a watchman – we think when he dies because 1795 is the date on the gravestone.

Why was he buried outside the churchyard?

Not yet known.

WW's date of death 1795 = the period when Merceron the church warden was doing lots of illegal stuff. Is there a link?

Is there a link between WW and Nathaniel Daykin? ND was executed several years before 1809 – was this around 1795? Did he know WW? Did he murder WW?

M was paying WW off because on M's orders he lied at the trial of Nathaniel Daykin.

See above. We don't yet know why M wanted ND dead.

Who is our ghost? ND? WW? Another watchman who was murdered by ND?

WW definitely.

Peter looked at the wall a little deflated. They had found out so much but still had so far to go. Mum and Dad however were looking more impressed. "We've done pretty well, our Peter!"

"It's amazing how living with a ghost makes you really want to get the job done!"

Caleb woke up from behind Dad's shoulder. "But we don't know why William lied do we?"

"We do know that actually," Peter retorted. "It's because he was in the pay of Merceron and was forced to do it."

"But if he was forced to do it, why did he get lots of money for it?"

The candle on the shelf flickered. Peter ignored it and his brother.

"The important thing now is to go through everything we know. I'm going to go through Professor Blackwell's papers, the church records and all the notes I've made again just in case we've missed something."

"And I'm going to clear the breakfast things away so we don't get marmalade on anything," Dad said gently pushing Caleb off his arm and standing up. "Then I'll start looking," he added in response to Peter's glare.

"I would help but I've got a call at 1030 with…" Mum had a strange look on her face as though she was split between loyalties. "Oh hang it. This is much more important. I'll cancel all meetings this morning."

"Caleb?"

"I'm tired. I'm going back to bed." (Caleb's interest in doing any work on the project waxed and waned like the moon.)

"I'll tell the watchman to haunt you!"

"You wouldn't!"

"Would!"

"Caleb!" Mum's voice had a definite edge.

"Okay, okay, keep your wigs on, I'll help!" Caleb shuffled back to the table. "What do I have to look at?"

Just then the phone rang. Dad took it into the lounge.

"Keep working chaps," Mum encouraged them. "Now we've started, it's important we don't get distracted."

A couple of minutes later he came back in. "That was the Rector." They looked up, surprised. "Now listen to me and don't say anything til you've heard me out. The police have finally come back to her to say that they are content for the skeleton to be reburied. So, the developer has made a decision to bury it back in its old grave. They are going to make the grave a bit of a feature of the new development - God knows how. And they're going to open the church to collect it and rebury it the day after tomorrow."

(That's if he's still there, worried Peter.)

There was a clamour of angry noise - the loudest this time from Mum.

"Tom, they can't do that! They've got to hear what we've found out."

Dad stood his ground. "Listen! I did tell the Rector that we'd worked out the identity of the ghost and that it meant that the skeleton needed to be buried in the churchyard. She sounded interested but said that the decision had been made and her hands were very much tied. I pushed her on this. She eventually said she would call a Zoom meeting with the Church Council tomorrow morning so we could tell them what we'd found out."

"Good work Dad." Seeing the strain on his father's face. Peter realised that Dad had won a hard-fought battle to get them this hearing.

"Well, we'd better get working then!" Caleb stood on top of the breakfast table and yelled, rather unnecessarily, at them. "COME ON - THERE'S NO TIME TO LOSE!"

CHAPTER 30

Razzy-Razzy-Rascal, you'd best budge up right now!

There's room on the sofa for both of us, and I need to read all this stuff that Pete has given me REALLY REALLY QUICKLY cos otherwise William the Watchman's skeleton will get buried BACK in the building site and they'll build a MASSIVE GREAT BLOCK OF FLATS on top of him and it'll be HORRIBLE and he'll end up haunting this house FOR EVER AND EVER.

And I'll grow up, and then get really old and wrinkly. And even when I've got a hearing aid and NO TEETH left and white hair growing out of my nose I'll still be haunted by him because no one will be able to find his grave EVER again because gazillions of people will be LIVING right on TOP OF IT!

And you'll hate that won't you! You can see him too and I know cos he makes your fur STAND ON END and you look really funny like your TAIL has been inflated, but it's not funny really because it's cos you're PROPER scared…

CHAPTER 31

He would never ever have admitted it but Peter was mightily impressed with his family that morning. Mum had brought her computer out of the pantry and was busy googling. Dad had taken the church records and, with the magnifying glass, was working through them line by line to see what they might have missed.

Caleb had been given Professor Blackwell's church history to read through the chapter on Merceron and King and to jot down any thoughts. This was not entirely helpful to the others.

"It says here that the local justice of the peace was in league with Merceron. Does that mean they played football against each other?"

"Shurrup Caleb!" Peter had taken Blackwell's bulky file and was carefully studying each entry.

"Leave him alone, Peter. Cay - it means that the local judge was being paid by Merceron to ignore all the bad things he was doing," Mum explained patiently.

Work continued in silence for a few minutes. Then there was a big huff and puff from Caleb.

"What's up now?" Dad said wearily.

"But how does Mr Blackwell know this stuff? I mean - he says here 'the Reverend King took evidence from Mistress de la Court, the mother of Nathanial Daykin' but how does he know that? He wasn't there, was he?"

"There'll be some kind of evidence to prove it - like a diary or a letter." Mum explained. "That's called primary evidence. It's something from the actual time to show what happened."

"Hang on – if Mr Blackwell mentions it in his book then he

must have had the evidence from somewhere - perhaps it's in this file." Peter upped his pace at checking every page and unfolding every document, trying to decipher both the ancient copperplate writing and Blackwell's scribbling.

They continued to work. Caleb quickly finished his chapter and Mum set him on reading the previous chapters in case anything was mentioned in that.

The clock ticked on. Caleb started humming as he read.

"Cay, if you make one more sound, I'll…!"

"Peter!"

But it was hard, hard, HARD. And very frustrating. The day was sunny and bright and, for April, promising to be a very warm one indeed.

At first Peter seized on every scrap of paper thinking that this might be the key to the mystery, but then it would turn out to be about buying gas lamps for the church grounds in 1865 or the colour of the choir's robes in the 1920s. By lunch time he had been through the file twice, had looked at everything carefully and could only conclude there was nothing left that could help them.

Across the table Dad was having the same trouble. No, correction, he was not. He had fallen asleep at some point in the early nineteenth century and was quietly snoring over the pages of the church records. Peter hoped he had not drooled onto the fragile pages. Mum and Caleb looked up at Peter's snort of laughter.

"Told you he'd be asleep!" Caleb went to wake their father up by wiggling the sleeper's ears.

"Gerroff our Caleb!"

"Did you dream the solution to the mystery, Tom?" Mum asked sarcastically while she started to make cheese on toast.

"Sorry." Dad pulled himself up to a sitting position and looked annoyed that he had been caught snoozing. "Now don't be hard on me - I have actually discovered a couple of things. Lay off Caleb!" He swatted his younger son on the arm to get him away. Peter and Mum looked at him. "Don't be so surprised - I can read you know. Anyway, what I did find were the funeral records of Nathaniel Daykin and that senior watchman, Samuel Weaver. Oh and I spotted the baptisms of Daykin and our William."

"That's majorly good work, Dad!" Peter said, impressed. Dad proudly showed them the entries in the parish record.

"Write them up on the Crime Wall" Mum commanded from the toaster. She handed out plates of cheese on toast and sat a large pot of apple chutney on the table. They sat munching, mulling over the new information.

"So poor old Nat Daykin was indeed fourteen when he died," Mum concluded. "Didn't it say somewhere he was executed on his fourteenth birthday?" She looked at her own nearly-fourteen-year-old with an odd expression.

"Not a good way to spend your birthday," Caleb pointed out sharply. "In fact, it's probably the worst birthday he'd ever had."

"And the last," Dad murmured.

"Especially if you were completely innocent," Peter said with feeling. The candle flickered.

They sat contemplating.

"And William was born in 1773," Mum asked, "or at least baptised then and I'm guessing they baptised the babies very soon after they were born?"

"How old was he when he died in 1795, Cay?" Dad asked, remembering his role as school master.

"Don't care." Caleb was not falling for that old trick of Making Him Do Maths When It Was Not School Work. He was looking over Dad's shoulders at the parish records.

"It does prove one thing," Mum recalled something.

"Remember the old rule about the unbaptised, suicides and lunatics not being allowed to be buried in a churchyard? Well – this information rules out William not being baptised as the reason he was buried on the other side of the wall."

The candle flickered again. This time with even more feeling. It was a very still day.

"Cay - make sure your hands are clean if you're going to look at those."

"They are!" Caleb hastily wiped them on his shorts. "What does '6s' and '6d' mean again? Didn't you say it was the old way of writing money?"

"Yes that's right."

"Because there's this list for 1794 of all the people who got buried in the church and next to their names there's money listed: look – 'Jacob Smith 6s, 6d,' - do you see?"

"Oh, that is interesting, Cay," Mum leant over to see. "I wonder if that's the fee people had to pay for a funeral."

"But look! Next to Samuel Weaver's name there's no money listed," Caleb proudly pointed out.

"Samuel Weaver got a free funeral?" Dad had pricked his ears up.

"Perhaps it was because he was a watchman - killed on duty or something," Peter said, interested despite the fact it was Caleb's discovery.

"Or perhaps someone felt guilty?" Mum said grimly.

The candle flickered furiously.

Caleb jumped up, took a fresh piece of paper, wrote his find out in big capitals, Blu-Tacked it onto the Crime Wall, and then helped himself rather smugly to the biggest apple in the fruit bowl. Mum was about to take a fruit as well but was interrupted by the strident tones of her phone.

"Bother, I'd better take this." She vanished into the pantry. They continued with the work.

"What's this?" Caleb was now fiddling with the lever-arch file.

"It's a lever arch file - people use them to file paper documents - don't break it. Have you honestly never seen one before?" Dad sighed. He dragged the file off him, opened it and demonstrated the mechanism that gave the file its name. "Now this file's a bit different from the type we had at my work. The back is much thicker than the front… hang on…" He fiddled with something. "Look - there's a compartment in the back cover. Did you check this, Pete?"

Immediately Peter jumped up and grabbed the file off him, cursing himself for missing it. Flinging open the file, he slammed forward all the pages he had read which had yielded nothing, and went directly to the back cover. Sure enough there was a thin slot across the top of the cover. He felt inside and was rewarded by finding a tatty cream slip. He fished it out carefully.

"Anything interesting?" asked Dad with a note of disappointment in his voice.

"Not sure," Peter replied studying it carefully. "What do you think?" He handed it over to Dad who peered at it for some time, as though trying to remember something.

"Do you know, Pete, I think it might be something like a library receipt - if you've borrowed a book or something. It says 'M.E.E.L' - can we google that to see if anything comes up?"

Caleb was already on to it; his quick fingers having seized Dad's phone.

"Got it! 'M.E.E.L stands for 'Museum of East End Life - I think that's near here!'".

Dad retrieved his phone quickly and looked at the map. "It's near Whitechapel Tube station – it must be only a few streets from here. So that means Mr Blackwell borrowed something from this museum for his book. But what?"

"The primary evidence!" Peter told them, starting to feel a little excited. "And I reckon I know what it was - look!"

Under the lettering M.E.E.L, someone had written:

'JB 18/2/18 Ltr dated 1809

Martha de la Court to Rev. King re son's death.'

There was a red stamp underneath the writing: *'RETURNED'*.

"Wasn't Nathanial's mum called Martha de la Court?" Peter jumped up and ran over to the Crime Wall, searching out the Post-it note he had stuck up all those weeks ago under Nathaniel Daykin's name. "Yes! It's got to be the letter Daykin's mum wrote to the Reverend King in 1809 complaining that Merceron had framed her son! Mr Blackwell must have borrowed the letter from the museum when he was writing the church history book. It's a shame he didn't photocopy it for the file because I bet it contains the missing information!"

Dad started to tap the table. "You could call the museum and see if they could track it down for you?"

Peter noted the number on the museum website and pressed it into his phone. They waited, watching him. He hung up quickly in disgust.

"No one there – the voice mail says they are all furloughed. That's a bit crap."

"May be Mr Blackwell can remember what the letter said?"

"But we can't tell Mr Blackwell about the ghost!" Caleb cried. "He'll think we're crazy and he wants to steal the skeleton!"

Peter looked at him in amazement. "How do you know that, Cay?"

"That night in the church - when he was taking all them photos of the skeleton. He was dead nosey. You didn't see him closely cos you were too busy looking at that gi… hey! Dad, Pete's just stepped on my toe!"

"Did not!"

"You did, you big fat liar!"

"Oh, just cut it out you two!" Dad had minimal patience when it came to fights.

"I'm going to be disabled now for the rest of my life," Caleb grumbled pathetically. He got out of his seat and limped slowly to the fridge to get some milk, wincing at every step. Peter felt a pang of guilt.

"Cay - do want to play footy? It's really sunny out there."

"Oh sure!" With a recovery faster than that of a Premiership footballer after the penalty's been awarded, Caleb grabbed his football and shot out of the house. Peter followed him, his mind thinking fast. It was vital that they found the letter - Peter was convinced it would have the answers they needed, but how to get it when it was locked up in a locked-down museum?

As he stepped out into the churchyard, realisation hit him like a glorious ray of sunshine.

This was most definitely a job for Felicity!

CHAPTER 32

You had to hand it to Caleb; you could completely rely on him for coming up with the weirdest of distractions!

Peter studied the results of his labour. If anyone glanced at it quickly, then it would pass for a local takeaway menu; by naming it the 'Great Northern Take Away' it should attract Felicity's attention and she would detect the concealed message inside. Switching his Bluetooth on, he sent the document to Mum's printer and then checked to see whether Dad was safely outside gardening. Then, nodding at Caleb to get into position, he slipped inside the bathroom to wait.

There was an anguished yowl from the lounge suggesting that a cat had been squirted with a water pistol, and then a louder and more tormented wail from Caleb as he put his acting skills to good use.

"Mum! MUUUUUUM! RAZZY'S GOT COVID!"

Oh man, why did he have to come up with that one? Still Mum might just fall for it and it would only take a few seconds… good. She was coming out of the pantry, grumbling and moaning, but on her way to the lounge… And now he was into the pantry and the printer was switched on so all he had to do was press print. And he could hear her talking to Caleb and then a quiet bit while she checked Razzy and then a louder bit when she started to shout at Caleb… Crap, she was coming back, print …print… it was printing… she was just at the pantry door!

No, she'd stopped. Caleb must have said something ridiculous to stop her in her tracks. She was shouting again, threatening to phone the RSPCA. It was printing – it was DONE!

Peter grabbed the paper and dashed out of the pantry, stuffing it in his pocket. Assuming a face of absolute innocence, he met Mum as she barged back into the kitchen, flushed and thoroughly unimpressed with his brother's antics.

"I tell you, Peter, I am deeply concerned about your brother! He's cooked up some absolutely ludicrous idea that the cat's ill with Covid!" Mum was almost feverish herself, she was so cross. "The cat's fine – Cay's been squirting him with his water pistol and feeding him crackers so of course the wretched thing's got a dry cough! Now, what's that strange condition people have where they make others ill for some attention? Do you think that it's the same condition if you make animals ill instead?" Still muttering to herself, she stomped back into the pantry and slammed the door.

Caleb poked his head around the kitchen door, grinning. "Did you get it printed?"

Peter beamed at his brother. "Sure thing. You've definitely earned me camping out with you when you do your cub camp. Anyway, let's go." They fled out of the front door, yelling to Dad in the garden that they were going for a walk. Peter strode off at such a pace that Caleb had to jog along to keep up.

"But how d'you know where this Felicity person lives?"

"Mr Blackwell's address was on the back of the file. It's not far - just in this next street."

They soon arrived at the house, a smart stone townhouse in a Georgian terrace that had somehow survived the Blitz. Peter looked at it nervously hoping his plan would work. It was cheeky but they only had one afternoon left to find this letter and desperate times meant desperate measures.

"Get ready to run, Cay!" He darted up to the blue front door, pushed the fake menu through and then rattled the door knocker loudly. He turned on his heels and they dashed to the safety of a nearby bus shelter where they could observe the door without been seen. The bus shelter had been in the direct sun all day and the red plastic bench was hot to touch. They crouched down as far as they could, straining to hear whether the door had been opened.

Soon voices could be heard in the quiet street – Peter was delighted to hear Felicity's among them. Surely she would at least look at the menu. The door closed abruptly and the street fell silent.

"Let's go." They left the bus shelter, pleased to be back in the fresh air.

"So what are you going to do now?" Caleb asked, panting like a small dog who is too hot.

"Go home, find an ice pop and sit in the shade somewhere!"

"Smart. So when is she supposed to meet you?"

"In ten minutes."

"Can I come with you?"

"Nope."

"Please?"

"Nada, nein, nyet, non. Absoluto no. No!"

"That's so not fair. I'll tell Mum I distracted her for you."

"Pete!!!!" There was a call behind them. They turned quickly and immediately Felicity was upon them. "Hey!" She gave a furtive look around and then gave Peter a quick kiss on the lips.

Peter smiled joyfully. "That was so quick!"

"Wow!" Caleb was staring at Felicity as if he had seen a vision.

"Hey Caleb!" Felicity called sweetly to him. She was wearing denim shorts and a pink checked shirt and had a flowery satchel slung around her. "How are you doing, my lovely?"

"I'm, uh, okay I guess."

Peter was amazed at Felicity's ability to stun his little brother into utter silence.

"Do you want to help us this afternoon?" Felicity turned to

face Caleb so that he got the full impact of her dazzling smile. "Caleb, would you be our alibi? You're a smart kid aren't you - you know what an alibi is? It's where you say that Peter has been with you all afternoon hanging out. Can you do that for us?"

Caleb nodded, dumbstruck.

"I brought these for you." Felicity reached into her satchel and brought out a small, insulated lunch bag. "Two Mars Bar ice creams. You'd better eat them quick before they melt. Come on, we'll drop you off at yours and you can tell your olds you're out in the churchyard with Pete."

Peter was seriously impressed how Felicity had already formed a plan for getting rid of Caleb even before she knew what was on the cards. And he could not believe how Caleb was rapturously drinking in every word she said to him, as though he were mesmerised.

"So what's the plan, Stan?" Felicity turned to him, her face shining with excitement. They had left Caleb at the Watch House and were walking back down the road.

"Let's walk," Peter told her. "I've got a few things to tell you but we are in a bit of a rush. Glad you worked out my message - and your note was epic! Love the invisible ink!"

The girl smiled. "That was me being brought up on those old children's books. You know - the Five Find Outers, Swallows and Amazons... Loved the name of your takeaway by the way!"

Peter smiled happily. "Didn't you just want to have a boat like Swallow?"

"After I read "Swallows and Amazons", I bugged my parents all summer to get me sailing lessons and they eventually did. They do lessons down at Shadwell Basin. We could do it together this summer - if they lift the lockdown."

"Oh I'd love to!" Peter had a picture of him and Felicity sailing gently down the Thames and out into the wide blue sea.

Felicity suddenly turned gloomy. "That's if Mum gets back okay."

"Why – where is she?"

"Barbados - my Nan lives out there now, and Mum went out in February to stay with her as she's not been too well. As I had school Mum said I couldn't go. So I had to stay here with Dad. Now Mum is stuck there because of lockdown. And I'm stuck with Dad and his mad plans to steal skeletons!"

"Don't you like your dad?"

"Oh he's an absolute idiot. One minute he's ridiculously strict on me like I can't even breathe without his permission; the next he's away in his precious little academic world and wouldn't notice if I held a massive house party in our kitchen!"

Peter could hear the bitter tone in her voice. He tried to change tack. "And your mum?"

"She's way out there as well but in a more reliable sort of way. She's a professor too - sometimes I call her "Professor Mummy". She's Head of Humanities at Queen Mary's and she's one of only twenty-six Black female professors in whole of the UK - which is a bit crap if you think about it. It means that she's got, like, this super-high profile and often has to go away to conferences around the world. But where are we going now?"

"To the Museum of East End Life. Do you know it?"

"Know it? I was practically brought up there! My parents used to take me there just about every weekend and Professor Mummy's a trustee. The curator's my Aunty Di – but she's ill in hospital at the moment with Covid." Felicity's voice saddened, but then she roused herself again. "But why do we need to go to the museum?"

Peter sighed. Where should he start? He stopped walking and turned to face Felicity. Suddenly he realised he was not intimidated by her anymore. She had told him about her family, time for him to tell her about his.

"This is a bit of a weird story - are you sure you want to hear it?"

"I thought we were in a rush?" Those gorgeous green eyes looked puzzled.

"We are, but you should hear this first and then you'll understand. And I promise you that every word of it is true."

So he told her the whole story. How the tree had destroyed their old house so that they'd moved to London just before lockdown. How they had found the skeleton, how the ghost began to appear. How they'd found out that the ghost was the skeleton - William Wadsworth, and how they had discovered William's terrible secret. How they really needed to persuade the church council to bury him in the churchyard - because the ghost kept appearing to them in all sorts of weird moods and, okay, he had not yet appeared in the bathroom, but just give him time. How they were still a bit clueless how to persuade the council because whichever way you looked at it, here was a man who had lied to get a kid put to death for a crime he did not commit.

"All my days!" For a moment Felicity was struck dumb. Peter went cold. Had he revealed too much? Was she now going to think him crazy?

But no, she lifted her head and looked straight at him with a look of exaltation. "So ghosts really do exist? That is, like, so amazing!"

"Well our one does. Who knows, you might even see him yourself."

"That's totally epic! And you figuring all that stuff out. You are one truly amazing person, Pete!"

Blushing deeply, Peter smiled, delighted. Then, pulling himself together, he explained about the tiny museum receipt. "And this is why we're here," he concluded as they rounded the corner to see the Museum of East End Life there in front of them.

"The meeting with the church council is tomorrow morning. I really think that this letter might hold the missing piece to the jigsaw."

Felicity was looking at the museum – an imposing sooty-red brick building standing at the end of a terrace. There was no sign of life. She turned to him, her eyes shining.

"Pete - I know exactly where that letter must be. In one of the rooms there's an exhibition all about bodysnatching for the Royal London Hospital. The room's stuffed with letters and documents from that time – all over the walls and in the glass cases. It's got to be in that room!"

"But how do we get in?"

They retraced their tracks, rounding the side of the museum until the rear of the terrace came into view. No smart façade here - the back of the museum was a mixture of odd-shaped windows bound together by the black metal of the fire escape. "Look!" Felicity whispered, pointing discretely. Halfway up the building a small window was open. "That's got to be our way in!"

CHAPTER 33

Hey Razzy-Razzy-Rascal, so you've come out here to be cool too? Smart plan you clever cat - it is SOOO LOVELY to lie here and look up at the sun through the leaves of the tree so it doesn't dazzle you!

Felicity and Peter eh!

That is so ABSOLUTELY AND UTTERLY HIL-AR-I-OUS !!! - our Pete having a girlfriend! A GIRLFIREND!!!!

I was right, Razzy, I was SO RIGHT cos I knew all those messages he was getting weren't from Granny! I could see it in his eyes!

And Felicity says it's my job to STAY HERE and give them an ALIBI - so that they can go and find that letter that Pete wants so much. Those ice creams were TOTALLY delicious - they really were. But I need my football Razzy. If I sneak in just now, I could always grab it quickly and come out again. If Mum catches me, I'll say Pete's waiting for me outside…

Oh crap, Mum just caught me! She was COMPLETELY INTERROGATING me as to why I had ice cream wrappers in my hands. It's NOT FAIR - if I was a COMPLETE MORON and just chucked them away anywhere then she wouldn't be able to ask questions. It's only because I'm being OH SO GOOD LITTLE CALEB and taking them to the bin in the kitchen that she SPOTS ME with them!

So I tell her that Pete found them in the freezer and that Dad must have bought them. And she NARROWS HER EYES and her lips PRESS TOGETHER like she does when she suspects something but has NO PROOF… But she then had a phone call and had to go back into her WITCH'S DEN, (cackle, cackle, cackle) so we are safe but only for now, because she WILL cross-examine Dad about the Bounty Bars. And he's TOTAL RUBBISH at standing up to her so he will give US AWAY immediately.

So here is my plan, Razzy. You and me are going to play footy in the churchyard just over the wall from where Dad is in the garden but where HE CAN''T SEE US AT ALL. I will call to me being Peter and I will say something back to Pete being me so that Dad will reckon we're BOTH there…

CHAPTER 34

Peter looked carefully around. Behind the museum, a small lane led off, connecting the back gardens of the terrace. The shadow cast from the terrace by the mid-afternoon sun set the entire row of gardens deep in blue shadow. He and Felicity slipped into the lane and stopped at the first gate – the gate that led into the museum's garden. It was about six foot high.

"Soon get over this!" Peter announced confidently. Using the gate's handle as a foothold, he pulled himself onto the top, swung his legs over and dropped off safely into the garden.

"Nicely done," remarked Felicity with a smirk as she entered the garden behind him via the gate which was unlocked. Peter flushed with embarrassment.

"Oh come on, Didiot!!" Felicity took him in her arms and kissed him again. "Don't you know that the more I like someone, the more I tease them! And it was quite funny, you've got to admit!" She broke away from him, giggling.

Peter found himself smiling at her infectious laugh. But Felicity's mind was now on higher things, and she was looking up at the open window.

"I reckon that's the second floor. If we can get in there, the room with the exhibition about bodysnatching is just along the corridor, so we won't have to go far. Now can we get onto the fire escape?" She twizzled a curl, thinking.

Peter traced the route of the black metal framework. "Look - there's a ladder at the far end." They ran over to where a rickety ladder met the ground, noting how it climbed precariously up the crumbling plaster wall up to intersect on each floor with an iron ledge which led under the row of museum windows.

"Race you!"

Peter grabbed the rungs first and started to clamber up the ladder, stopping when he realised that each movement sent up a terrible clanking noise that echoed off the surrounding buildings. "Crap," he whispered to Felicity below him, "we're making a right noise. I'd best go steady!"

He set off again, this time slowly and carefully, climbing as stealthily as a cat, soon reaching the level of the open window. Leaving the safety of the ladder, he worked his way across the narrow ledge. He was rather high up now and the ledge was comprised of a see-through metal grid; he took comfort from the fact that a handrail attached to the brickwork ran the whole distance. Moving carefully along, he eventually reached the open window and realised thankfully that he could fit through. He was about to do so when a thought struck him.

"Hey Fliss, will the alarm be on?"

She had arrived by his side on the ledge and shook her head. "Don't know. I suspect it might be, but I know the code if it is. I guess I'll just have to race down the stairs to get to the control panel in time to switch it off. The panel's by the reception desk at the front."

"You'd better go first then," Peter started to move aside and then stopped. "How the heck do you know the code?" he asked her, bewildered.

"Aunty Di is totally obsessed with Elizabeth the First." Felicity laughed. "She's told Mum loads of times that she uses the date of Elizabeth's death as the alarm code - 1603."

Peter had another thought. "D'you think she'll mind us breaking into her museum?"

"Don't worry - I promise I'll tell her when she's better. She'll get what we're trying to do and she'll think it's the best story in the world. She's like that, a bit obsessed but totally chilled about everything. Now, Peter my lovely, we can't hang about here all day - sunny as it is!" Felicity managed to get a leg over the windowsill and swung herself over. "I'll go in really slowly and if the alarm goes off, I'll run like hell to switch it off! Wish me luck!"

Peter waited, watching as Felicity dropped cautiously down from the sill and into the room. She started to move forward, each footfall poised, ready to spring into action. The room was long but narrow, glass cases running along each side. As she made it successfully to the middle, she stopped and beckoned him in.

'It's okay, Pete, the alarm doesn't appear to have been set or I would have triggered it by now. Bit weird it's not been set though. Maybe the sensor in this room isn't working?"

"Or perhaps someone else's in the building and has switched it off?" Peter had a horrible thought as he wriggled through the window. Although the room was cool and dark, he felt himself sweaty with nervousness.

"Well, the bodysnatching display's not far away - we won't be long," Felicity smiled reassuringly and gently took him by the hand. They crept through the room and paused at the door, which was slightly ajar. Still fearful of the alarm, they gently pushed the door open and stepped through. But again nothing happened.

They were now standing in a larger room with a wide entrance at the far end through which the main staircase could be seen. Peter breathed a sigh of relief. Felicity joggled his hand jubilantly. "So, I reckon the alarm's not set as it would definitely have gone off by now. Let's get what we need as quickly as possible. Now if I remember right, we need to go this way."

She led him past the staircase and turned right down a narrow windowless corridor. Peter followed, increasingly uneasy at being inside a museum when it was closed. It was not so much that they were breaking in, he reasoned, it was something more than that. The absence of bright lights and friendly staff made the place feel very strange. He suddenly recalled Caleb-the-Toddler throwing memorable tantrums whenever they went to a museum, and now had an inkling why.

"So," whispered Felicity pointing at a pale green door at the end of the corridor. "That's the room with the display on the body snatchers. Do you want to go in first?"

Feeling like this was some sort of test, Peter slipped passed her and pushed the door open. He gave a gasp of surprise - there staring at him was the Watchman! Yes, William the Watchman in his proper uniform - from his tricorn hat to his big black boots and his rattle! He felt a bolt of adrenaline shoot through him and his heart began to beat furiously.

But no, oh man - he felt a proper twerp! It was a mannequin dressed up as a watchman of the period, designed to welcome visitors to the exhibition. He forced out a laugh.

"He got me for a moment!"

"Oh of course, the watchman dummy! I'd forgotten about him. Is that what your ghost looks like?"

"Just about, except this one's better looking!" As soon as the words were out of his mouth he regretted them, feeling weirdly disloyal. He looked nervously around. Might William turn up here as well? Probably not, he thought. William seemed to stick to the paths he had taken when alive. The museum building, though possibly from the right time, must have been a rich person's house and not for the likes of William.

He pulled himself together and started to look around the exhibits. Despite his nervousness, the sheer amount of material about the bodysnatching entranced him and he wished he'd had access to this room all along. The walls and cases were teeming with information about the Age of Enlightenment and the desire for dead bodies from the surgeons at the Royal London; he read with interest how every surgeon with a reputation to build wanted a body to dissect (and was willing to pay handsomely) and that the Church was, unsurprisingly, wholly against the idea. Hence the grim yet lucrative business of breaking into churchyards after dark.

In a corner, to his delight, there was actually a display about the bodysnatching at St Wilfred's. There was a dignified portrait of the Reverend King, and a vivid description of the skulduggery of Merceron. Yellowing under a glass plate, there was the original transcript from Nathanial's trial, and next to it, a letter. Excited, he bent over the glass to read the narrow writing. It was indeed the missing letter – from Martha de la Court to the Reverend King!

Feeling completely vindicated, he pulled out his phone and took a photo. Then he called Felicity over. "D'you reckon we can open this case? I really need to turn the letter over so I can copy the whole thing.

"Sure. Let's see if the glass lifts up." She carefully placed her fingers into the corners of the glass plate and eased it upwards. To their delight, it came up easily and then:

BRRRRRRRRRRRRRRRRRRRRRRRRRRRRRRRRRRRR!!!!!!!!!!!!!!!
!!!!!!!!!!!!!!!

Crap, crap, crappity crap!

Felicity froze, glass now clear from the box and shouted at Peter over the din. "Quick, take your photo and let's get out of here!"

Reaching into the box, Peter managed to turn the precious letter over so that the underside was revealed. Then he quickly took the photo, shoved his phone into his pocket, and put the letter back, placing it deftly back onto the canvas backcloth in line with the dust outline. Felicity, with admirable control, placed the glass back onto the lid of the display case.

Mercifully, the alarm ceased.

"Got your photos? Let's go!" Felicity dashed out of the room. Peter followed her, slightly regretful that he could not stay and look at the rest of the exhibition. He ran back through the green door out through the corridor to the stairs, and then stopped dead in his tracks.

At the top of the stairs Felicity was standing. Directly behind her, a man stood, pining her arms behind her so that she could not move from his grasp!

CHAPTER 35

Dad was having a very strange experience. Working hard re-potting lettuces in their small but busy backyard, he was listening to Caleb's voice as it drifted over the wall to him, punctuated by the sound of a football hitting the wall.

Caleb (with voice sounding at his normal pitch): "Nice shot, Pete."

Caleb (with voice sounding as a low growl): "Cay, that's a rubbish shot. A monkey with its legs tied together could kick the ball better."

Caleb (normal): "It's cos you've moved, dummy!"

Caleb (growly voice): "I only moved so that the sun's not in my eyes, you arch-moron!"

And so on.

Eventually Dad could concentrate on his lettuces no longer. Cautiously he climbed up onto the rim of the raised bed to look over the wall to see what exactly Caleb was up to. He watched silently as his son kicked the ball against the wall, alternating the voices and coming up with more ludicrous insults as he did so.

"Cay?"

The boy gave a startled whimper and looked up. "Dad, you totally scared me!" He looked round for the ball, found it and clutched it to his chest.

"But what are you doing?"

"Playing footy."

"Yes I can see that. But where's Peter?"

A look of sheer panic swept across Caleb's brow.

"Erm, he's gone for a run…"

"Has he now." Caleb's face screamed guilt at him. Peter was not known for his enthusiasm for running.

"I think he asked Mum if he could go," Caleb added desperately. "Can I carry on playing footy?"

"Why don't you and I have a little walk to see if we can meet him coming home from his run?" Dad suggested, taking off his gardening gloves. "I could do with a leg stretch. Now which direction did he say he was going?"

Caleb pointed miserably in the direction of the museum.

"Right. Meet me at the front door and, whatever you do, don't disturb your mother."

CHAPTER 36

Peter stood motionless, staring in horror at the scene in front of him.

The man holding Felicity was very odd looking. Tall and skinny, he had bushy unkempt hair and a scraggy grey beard, topped with a grubby flat cap. Scrawny freckled arms protruded out of a polo shirt which was emblazoned with the museum logo. He appeared to be a museum security guard – but why did the man appear so neglected? And why was he holding Felicity like a prize?

The man saw Peter and growled. "Another one! What're you doing in my museum?"

Felicity, despite her obvious discomfort, was trying to remain cool and collected. "It's okay Pete - this is Kenneth. He's the security guard at the museum." She tried to turn her head so that the man could see her face. "Hi Kenneth, please can you let go of me? You know me, I'm Professor Moore's daughter - we've met loads of times. This is my friend Pete. I'm sorry we freaked you out. We were just checking out something for a history project - we weren't stealing anything, I promise we weren't."

The man didn't appear to be listening. The sight of intruders seemed to have triggered something in his brain. He looked at them strangely, his baby-blue eyes seeming out of focus. He drew Felicity closer to him, one arm locking her arms firmly around her back, the other clasped tightly onto her mouth. Felicity was now wide eyed - Peter could see she was trying to take long breaths so as not to panic.

What could he do? He tried to smile reassuringly at Kenneth while his mind raced round and round for a plan. He first considered phoning the police - but dismissed that idea immediately. His parents? Dad would panic and Mum would go up the wall. No, he was not going to do that!

The glimmer of an alternative plan started to rise in his mind. It might just work...

Ever so slowly so not to spook the man, Peter pulled his phone out from his pocket. He held it up so it could be seen and, after a quick calculation as to the current time in Barbados, said clearly "Siri, call Queen Mary's College, London." He heard the connection being made and the dialling tone. He waited, still trying to maintain eye contact with Felicity and her captor until a voice answered the call.

"This is Queen Mary's. How can I help you?"

Keeping his eyes on the man's face, he spoke in his most polite grown-up voice. "Can I be transferred to Professor Moore please? It's urgent, it's about her daughter."

There was a longer pause until a voice came on the other end of the voice, deep and mellifluous, sounding slightly anxious. "This is Angela Moore. How can I help you?"

"Erm, hi there. I'm Peter Ashby - I'm a friend of Felicity's - don't worry, she's not hurt or anything, but we need your help."

The voice changed to one of recognition.

"You're Peter! *The* Peter? The one my daughter hasn't stopped going about?"

"Um, I guess so." Peter felt himself redden again. Was Felicity now giggling behind the man's hand or was it his imagination?

The voice laughed exuberantly. Peter had a vision of an adult Felicity, triumphant and gorgeous.

"Well Peter-the-often-spoken-about, what on earth's going on?"

"I'm sorry to disturb you but we're, erm, in the Museum of East End Life and we've met this security guard Kenneth and he's holding Felicity and there's no one else around. Can you talk to him please?"

Peter stopped, hoping she would not ask any questions or query why they were hanging around a museum that was locked up and out of bounds. After what seemed like an eternity the voice spoke again, calm, authoritative but friendly.

"Of course. I know Kenneth. Might I speak with him?"

"Sure." He held the phone out. Kenneth stared at it, puzzled, as though he had never seen a phone before.

"Good day to you Kenneth. How are you doing? It's Angie Moore here – remember me, Di's friend? Now, I saw you last at the museum Christmas party and I was telling you all about how we make Roti in Barbados. I was going to cook a special dish of it for you, remember?"

The man muttered something.

"Well, I am sorry not to have brought it over to you, but, because of this Covid business, I'm stuck out here in Barbados. But as soon as I'm back in London, I promise you I'll bring a dish round. Are you living at the museum at the moment? Keeping it safe for Di?"

The man thought. "Yes I am. It's very safe."

"That's great Kenneth. Diana must be mightily relieved to have you there as she knows you do a really good job. Now, if my daughter Felicity is with you there, can you let her know if there's anything you need?"

"I guess I will." At this the man seemed to wake up to the fact that he was still holding Felicity. Without another word, he abruptly let go, and Felicity staggered away from his clutches, rubbing her arms. Gently, Peter put his arm around her. She was shaking.

"I'm okay Mum," Felicity called out in as composed a voice as possible. "Kenneth has let go of me now so we're going to be fine."

"Thank you, Kenneth," the voice continued, still calm but clearly relieved. "Felicity and Peter are going to leave you now but thank you again for your hard work."

The man grunted – whether he was happy or not for them to go, they could not tell. Peter led Felicity slowly passed Kenneth, towards the room with the open window. He held the phone out so Kenneth could see they were still connected.

"Thanks Professor Moore. Fliss and me are leaving now…"

They left the staircase and walked carefully towards the room with the open window. Feeling Kenneth's eyes on their backs, Peter tried not to hurry, fighting a desperate urge to flee. As they reached the room, they shut the door quickly behind them with a bang and raced over to the open window.

"You go first," Peter told Felicity. Without another word she was out of the window, onto the iron walkway and down the ladder as fast as a cat fleeing a dog. She reached the bottom and looked up.

"Is he following us, Pete?"

"Nope - no sign of him." Peter followed her out of the window and soon was standing next to her in the museum garden. He handed his still-connected phone over to her.

"Mum you were freakin' amazing!" Felicity burst into tears and sank down on a bench. Peter stood slightly away from them, not wanting to butt in, yet trying to figure out how to persuade Felicity to move to the street where they would no longer be trespassing. Felicity however pulled him over to her.

"Peter, that was an absolutely chill idea to call Mum!"

From his phone's speaker, Professor Moore's voice echoed the praise. "Thank you, Peter. I'm sorry that little minx of mine is getting you into trouble."

"It's okay Professor, it was my idea…" Peter realised that he didn't know where to start. He suddenly remembered, with a pang of guilt, that Caleb would be waiting for them.

Thankfully Felicity had dried her eyes. "Mum, we've really got to go. Talk to you later – on Zoom again because I haven't found my phone yet. Love you!"

As she handed his phone back, she stood up, stretching her arms and wriggling her shoulders. "All my days! That was scary wasn't it!"

"If you're feeling better, shall we get out of the garden? I'm just a bit worried in case Kenneth calls the police."

"I'm not sure he'll do that." They walked out into the back lane. "I can remember him now - he's been working as a security guard for the museum for years and years, but he's usually very well dressed and friendly. I wonder what's happened?"

"There's definitely something odd going on there." Peter was trying to get Felicity to walk faster without making it obvious. "When I called the museum just after lunch, it said that all its staff were on furlough…"

He had suddenly spotted Dad and Caleb ahead of them. Grabbing Felicity by the arm, he pulled her into an alley way between two buildings.

"What are you doing?" Felicity looked alarmed.

"Wanted one last kiss!" He could hardly believe he was asking her.

"Honestly!" Felicity chided him, mocking. She kissed him gently but swiftly and they broke off smiling at each other.

"Now are we still on for tonight?"

Felicity looked bewildered for a moment and then the light dawned in her eyes. "Oh course! We've got to stop my Dad skelly-stealing! But before then, I think I should talk to Mum about Kenneth because I really think he needs help."

"You're one amazing lass, Fliss!" Peter was struck by her care for her attacker.

"You are too, Peter the Great – oh please let me call you that! It really seems to fit."

"I'm not complaining!" He beamed at her, gratified. "Now I've really got to go!

CHAPTER 37

So Razzy-Razzy-Rascal, me and Dad start walking down the road and I'm trying to walk slowly and do all this CLEVER STUFF like pretending my shoelace is undone so I can slow him down. And I can tell that Dad knows BIG TIME that something is going on cos he's got this WORRIED WIGGLY LINE running across the top of his face - and also because he realises that I'm wearing VELCRO trainers which DON'T HAVE LACES so he gets cross with me and tells me to stop being AN IDIOT and wasting time.

And I say: 'don't worry, Pete will be fine. He's not been gone long'. And Dad ignores me, which is a good thing really because Pete's actually been gone for HOURS AND HOURS AND HOURS and if he starts asking me stuff like where he actually went I'm going to run

out of ideas really really quickly. So I KEEP QUIET which makes Dad FROWN even more.

And then THANK GOD we see Pete coming towards and he is ON HIS OWN! But then I realise that Peter won't know that Dad thinks he's been OUT FOR A RUN. So just as we get close, I slip behind Dad and do SLOW MOTION RUNNING while pointing to Pete and mouthing 'you'. And then suddenly Dad turns back to look at me so I have to turn the 'you' into a howl and PRETEND to be a wolf. And Dad looks at Pete and Pete looks at Dad in a 'what on earth is Cay doing' usual type of way and I'm pleased cos Dad won't BE MAD with Pete anymore.

And Pete says: 'hi guys, I've been for a run,' and I sneak him a thumbs up to show him that he's understood. And he does look HOT AND SWEATY and he is wearing trainers and shorts and PONGS a bit so that he does actually look like he's been for a run. And Dad says 'okay then, but next time tell me, understood?' And Pete says 'understood'.

And then I remember about the letter and I am really DYING to ask him if he found it. But I can't ask him of course until we get home and Dad has put the kettle on and has gone to ask Mum if she wants a cup of tea – which she does of course and is now in a BETTER MOOD and ACTUALLY (AND UNBELIEVABLY) believes Pete when he says he went for a run.

So I ask Pete whether he got the letter and then Dad (who has gone the most SENSITIVE EARS IN THE WHOLE UNIVERSE) pricks his ears up and asks 'what letter?' And Pete, without going red or anything which is quite an AMAZING accomplishment for him, says COMPLETELY QUICKLY that he met Professor Blackwell out while running and told him about FINDING the receipt for the letter and Professor Blackwell said he HAD GOT IT, and that on his way home he stopped at the Professor's house and the Professor brought the letter out for him so that he could take a photo of it.

And Pete is telling so many FIBS now that Dad looks a little bit groggy, like he has been hit on the head with a FRYING PAN. But I remind Dad that the letter is TOTALLY AND UTTERLY IMPORTANT as it might tell us why the horrible church warden killed Nathanial and what our William had to do with it, and that it PROBABLY ALMOST DEFINITELY will be evidence for the council meeting tomorrow.

And then it FINALLY dawns on Dad that he REALLY REALLY wants to know what's in the letter as much as we do, so we sit down, and he stops INTERROGATING Pete, and brings his cup of tea over.

CHAPTER 38

Despite the afternoon's excitement at the museum, Peter could not believe how much his heart was racing as he opened his phone to find the photos of the letter. Recalling that the second photo had been taken under rather trying conditions, he scanned them anxiously. Thankfully he could see the writing clearly on both.

Surely, he told himself sternly, no one in the world has ever been so excited about a two-hundred-year-old letter. It is simply not possible. But with Dad and his brother waiting expectantly at the kitchen table, and Caleb's fervent belief in the letter bearing all the answers they needed, he began to read out loud.

"Wardlaw Court

Spitalfields

15th March, the Year of our Lord 1809.

To the Reverend Joshua King

I am writing to set before you the most grievous charge against the Church Warden of St Wilfred's, Joseph Merceron. I write nothing but the truth when I tell you he is entirely responsible for the death of my son, Nathaniel Daykin.

Nathaniel was born in 1780. My first husband, Nathaniel's father, was a skilled stone mason and was often away around the country courted for his talents. But he earned a good wage and we were happy.

Joseph Merceron and I had known each other from childhood. It is true to say that I did not like him even when he was a little boy. He was manipulative and vicious and would use his family's influence to force others to do wrong - a practice that he has not grown out of. But the worst of it was that he wanted me for his wife and I refused him and he made my life very unpleasant. When I married my husband I was glad to be away from that place and felt myself safe in London. But it was not to be.

When our son Nathaniel was twelve, he was apprenticed as a mason. One day coming home he came across an older youth being cruel to two small boys. My son called his fellow apprentices and they beat that youth and sent him packing. The youth was Merceron's son.

When Merceron realised that his son's chief assailant was my son, he tracked us down. It was one of those periods when my husband was away. To my horror, it turned out that he was the landlord of our lodgings and indeed of my husband's workshop. He treated me vilely and told me that if ever anything happened to my husband, I must promise to marry him, else he would evict me and have my boy in front of the magistrates for attempted murder of his son. What could I do but promise and trust to God that my husband had good health and would return soon.

Alas but within a few months after that I received a letter to tell me that my husband had been killed while working on the minster in York. It was a terrible shock and Nathaniel and I grieved sorely. We were lucky though to have a good friend in our neighbour, Francis de la Court, whom we had known for many years. Francis worked for one of London's merchant houses. He began to pay me attention and we were soon wed.

Francis had to go abroad on business. While he was absent, Merceron came back to find he had missed his chance. He was not able to evict me as I was now a merchant's wife and safe in my new husband's house. But he took out his revenge on my son.

On the morning of the ninth of June, we were woken by loud hammering on the door. It was the local Watch with a warrant for the arrest of Nathaniel. My boy went willingly, with the innocence of youth, assuming it was a mistake. But he was charged with the murder of a watchman and before we knew it, he was in court facing the judge.

Now I have learned since that Merceron has considerable influence with the local justices and with the Watch, and so it proved that morning. He was able to produce a watchman who claimed that he had seen my son enter St Wilfred's' churchyard, with the intent to body snatch and that his fellow watchman had been killed by Nathaniel as he tried to apprehend him.

I stood up in the court and shouted that this was all a lie and that my son had been at home sleeping all night long. But Merceron produced another witness to state that I had business on the streets that night and could not have known. (I might add, sir, that this was a damnable lie - my husband and neighbours will bear witness that I am a respectable woman.) And so my son was found guilty of murder and was hung the next morning. I was allowed a short visit to say goodbye and begged my boy's forgiveness for not marrying Merceron. But my boy was as good as he was innocent and told me that I would have had a wretched life married to that man. We bade farewell and promised that we would meet again in Heaven.

A month later my husband came home. My boy had been buried at Newgate prison. Francis had him reburied in the churchyard in a proper grave. It was all he could do. He has vowed that one day, when he has made his money he will seek revenge on Merceron. I cannot tell you when that will be because he has been away now for several years and I am not sure if he is still alive.

Reverend King, you must believe me when I tell you that I have tried to forgive Joseph Merceron but it has proven impossible to do so. His evil doings have implicated others - the watchman, Wadsworth, who gave the evidence that condemned my son, killed himself with his own blunderbuss not so long afterwards – another soul destroyed!

There are also rumours, mere rumours I add this time, that the *watchman Weaver killed in the churchyard that night was killed at the command of Merceron - for what reason I cannot tell you other than to frame my son.*

Sir, you will now have read this testimony of an honest woman. I beseech you to hold Joseph Merceron to account for his crimes.

Yours truly

Martha de la Court."

Feeling rather stunned, Peter looked up from his phone and at Dad and Caleb. They were staring at him in absolute silence. A stray thought flashed through his mind that Dad might still be mad at him, but then realised they were not looking at him but to something beyond him. He spun round.

There, in the doorway, the Watchman stood with tears rolling down his miserable grey face.

It was Caleb who moved first. He got off his chair and moved towards the phantom, his arm outstretched as though trying to pacify a worried dog. "Hey Mister William, don't cry. We know you didn't mean to do it. We're on your side."

But as he drew close the ghost promptly evaporated, and Caleb found himself stroking thin air.

CHAPTER 39

Peter sat down to catch his breath. The frustrations of the morning seemed a lifetime ago; he could hardly believe it was the same day. And he still had to come up with a plan to escape to meet Felicity that evening.

Caleb and Dad were filling the Crime Wall with the new information - a satisfying process given that they now had so many more of the jigsaw pieces – and Mum was sitting at the kitchen table being brought up to speed. Having printed out Martha's letter, (she had neither inquired about its fortuitous appearance, nor had anyone told her) she finished reading it and sighed.

"So there we have it. Nathaniel Daykin executed on Merceron's orders simply to get revenge on Martha de la Court because she refuses to marry him. William Wadsworth commits perjury at Nathaniel's trial under Merceron's orders and then kills himself because he can't live with the shame. And because he kills himself, he's not allowed to be buried in the churchyard. Poor old William!"

"He didn't half look upset when we saw him last," Dad agreed.

"No wonder. He's a restless soul with the death of this entirely innocent boy on his conscience." She swallowed her tea, her voice cracking with emotion.

"Mum, you're crying again." Caleb told her.

"Am not." She took a tissue surreptitiously from her sleeve and blew her nose.

"But what can we do?" Peter wrestled his mind away from meeting Felicity to deal with another question that had been bothering him. "I mean, we now know that he lied at the trial, took money for lying and then killed himself because he was so ashamed…"

"Shush, Peter, he might be listening." Caleb pointed his finger out towards the hallway. Peter ignored him.

"But that doesn't help our case that he should be buried in the churchyard, does it?"

"I don't know," Mum said thoughtfully. "Mrs de la Court's letter shows us that Merceron was a deeply unpleasant character. William was young, and poor and in his pay, so he was just carrying out orders. I've a strong suspicion he lied because he had to - because he would have been fired or worse." Mum picked up the letter again and pointed to the concluding paragraph. "I mean, look at this: Mrs de la Court hints that Merceron had the old watchman, Samuel Weaver, killed as part of the plot to frame Nathaniel!"

"So you're saying that we can now build a much more sympathetic case for William to be buried in the church yard," Peter looked at her. "Despite him having killed himself?"

"Yes - when we meet with the church council tomorrow morning, we can present them with the evidence to try and persuade them. Given that the law has now changed, we should at least have a chance."

Peter went back to figuring out how to escape to join Felicity. Could he use Caleb as a decoy again? No - although he figured that Caleb would be thrilled to be given another chance to act up, Mum was growing increasingly suspicious of her younger son's behaviour.

Dad on the other hand was watching Peter's own behaviour like a rather nosey hawk. Hmm - what to do? If he started being too helpful, Dad would be rather sceptical…

In the end it was the evening's glorious sunset that gave him the solution. After they were clearing up after tea, (Teriyaki salmon with Udon noodles - Dad was branching out,) Peter looked out of the window to see the windows of the flats opposite illuminated with vivid streaks of pink and orange.

"Mum, I'm going to pop out to the churchyard with my phone - I want to try a new photo-filter app to see if I can get some good shots of the sunset. Don't tell Dad cos I had to pay three quid for it, and I put it on his credit card."

Mum nodded, understanding. "Good luck - hope it works."

"Thanks – I'll probably be out some time as I might try and get some photos of the graves as it gets dark."

"That's fine. Remember to take your jacket so you don't get cold."

Peter grinned and grabbed his dark grey hoodie and then he was free! Free to rush out into the churchyard on his own. It was only a quarter to eight, but the Professor was already in the church as he could hear the sound of the organ. He sauntered down the yard's tree-lined pathways, relishing the coolness of the evening.

As he wandered under a particularly fine London plane tree, he felt a small twig strike his ear and then another. He looked up abruptly and was met with a hissed whisper.

"Don't look up at me, Didiot! Pretend you haven't seen me, walk on, then double back and climb up."

Within a couple of minutes, Peter was sitting in the tree next to her.

"Hey Fliss!" he grinned.

"Hey Peter-the-Great!" She smiled at him, a genuinely happy smile and kissed him. Then she cuddled up to him and he felt a glow of happiness feeling her warmth next to him, relieved that she appeared fully recovered from the afternoon's ordeal.

"So what's happening?"

The evening sunshine made her green eyes shine like a tiger's. Laughing quietly, she sat up, now absolutely alert.

"So. Dad's in church practising the organ but his friend Maurice is outside in his big snazzy Range Rover ready and waiting for Dad to call him. When it's dark, they are going to steal the skeleton. That's their plan anyway when I listened into their call this evening on the upstairs extension. Never make evil plans using a landline, chaps!" She waggled her finger at a surprised blackbird, who promptly flew off."

"Has he found the skeleton then?"

"Don't know exactly, but he hasn't brought anything out yet. I figured there would be time for us to slip in while he's distracted playing the organ."

"How come he hasn't brought you with him tonight?"

"Because he wants to steal the skeleton, Didiot, and has got enough nous to realise I might stop him!" Felicity pushed herself off the branch and swung down the trunk gracefully.

Yes, Felicity was definitely back on form, Peter thought ruefully, as he clumsily clambered down after her, feeling like he had grown extra limbs.

Running up the steps to the door, they paused to make sure that the organ playing was in full flow and then slipped in and hid behind the font in Caleb's niche. It gave a good view of the tomb of Sir Percival. By now the sun had set and the church's interior was cast in deepening shadows. At the far end they could see the back of Felicity's father, silhouetted against the light of the lamp on the organ console. He was playing something loud and complicated that reverberated around the building.

Under cover of the music, Peter felt he could risk a whisper.

"So why are we actually here? Just to make sure they don't find the skelly and to try and stop them if they do?"

To his surprise, Felicity suddenly sounded rather embarrassed. "Well yes, but... erm, you know I lost my phone? Well I...er...might have left it in the tomb where we hid the skeleton."

"You're joking!" Peter put his hand to his mouth so that he didn't laugh out loud.

Felicity pretended to be hurt. "It's not that funny! I was…a bit distracted, wasn't I?"

He grinned broadly. "Now who's the 'Didiot'?"

"Stop it!" But she smiled back at him, her eyes laughing. "I was hoping that after Dad's gone, you might help me with the tomb lid so I can check inside - and make sure the skelly's okay of course."

"Course I will." Peter wriggled around to give Felicity some space. She snuggled up to him again.

"So we've just got to play the waiting game."

That was absolutely fine by him, he could quite happily stay in their hiding place all night. They sat listening to the music as the shadows around them steadily grew. Was there a tune? Peter tried in vain to find one, but just as he thought he could catch a melody, it disappeared again in a confusion of notes.

Beneath the sound of crashing chords Felicity raised her mouth to his ear. "I had a long chat with Mum this evening - told her all about the ghost and your detective work and everything. She was completely fascinated about the whole thing. Do you mind if she puts something on her blog?"

"Oh, yes. Sure." In this delightful state of being he would happily agree to anything.

"Oh and she's contacted the other trustees about Kenneth. It's really sad. The whole museum staff were furloughed back in March, but it looks like Kenneth, for some reason, has been living on his own in the museum - must have got confused or something and thought he was doing his job by guarding it so well. Thank God the museum café was so well stocked – that's how he's been able to survive. Anyway - they've contacted Social

Services."

Peter, remembered the obvious signs of neglect, realised something with a pang of guilt. "Oh man, we must have totally scared him!"

"You bet we did. But it just shows you how this crappy lockdown is really affecting vulnerable people. I mean, who's watching out for folk like Kenneth? Not people like my dad, who's just obsessed with how it's affecting his stupid research!"

Recalling what Professor Blackwell had said last time they met, Peter had a sudden revelation. "Who watches the watchmen!"

She looked at him, bemused so he tried to explain.

"It's what your dad said about who guards the guards. A security guard's a watchman, isn't he? All this time we've been worried about William the Watchman when there was a real-life watchman who desperately needed our help."

He suddenly felt an awful lot better about having broken into the museum if it meant that Kenneth was to be given the care he needed. Felicity took his hand in hers and squeezed it affectionately.

The organ music reached a thunderous crescendo and then ceased. The silence slammed down on them and Peter found himself almost reeling. Blackwell rose from the organ console and fussed around changing his shoes and organising his music. They wriggled deep into their hiding place, Peter realising with a jolt of panic that if Blackwell went all over the church with a torch, he would be bound to find them.

The light on the organ console went off and the place plunged into darkness. They watched as Blackwell's torch light moved out of the chancel and over to the north side of the nave, stopping at the tomb of Sir Percival.

Making sure that his own phone was on silent and buried deep in his pocket, Peter held his breath. He sensed that, next to him,

Felicity was doing the same.

Then the professor gave a shout of annoyance. They could see the light darting here and there as he started to search high and low for the missing skeleton. Peter grinned happily in the dark. Let him look, he would never find him!

Now the light, on its most powerful setting, shone around the nave like a search light in an old war movie; at one point it came perilously close and Peter was glad of his dark hoodie. They sat motionless, waiting for the light to pass, which it did. The font did its duty and guarded them well.

Eventually the light dwindled down to a tiny square held close to the man's face as he made a call. "Hello Maurice. No. There's no sign of it - the Rector must have moved it without telling me. Yes, very annoying I know. No, you head home. Thanks for your efforts - much appreciated. Sorry it's been a complete waste of your time."

They ducked once more into their hiding place as Blackwell passed them heading for the church door. They heard him set the alarm and then lock the door firmly.

Then he was gone.

CHAPTER 40

Felicity slipped out of their hiding place and dashed over to the door to switch the alarm off. Then she danced jubilantly down the dark aisle. "He's gone, he's gone! The skeleton's safe! Take that, you villain, with your dastardly plan!"

Peter followed her out, feeling the stiffness in his legs. "Hang on Fliss - how are we going to get out now your Dad's locked the door?"

"Oh don't worry - the fire door in the vestry has one of those bars on it so that you can get out."

Peter relaxed. "So, we hid William well!" It was his turn to laugh with glee.

"William?"

"The skelly."

"Of course! Sorry, I'm being a bit dense! I'm just so happy we thwarted my Dad!"

Remembering what she had said that afternoon about her father, Peter felt sorry that Felicity felt this way. His own father could be pretty annoying, but it would be a little extreme to label him as a villain – despite what Caleb reckoned when he was in a bad mood.

Sounding eery from inside the church, the clock chimed the half hour. Peter glanced at the long windows and decided that he did not have to rush straight back. There was still a glimmer of twilight left in the sky for him feasibly to be out in the churchyard taking photos.

"Shall we find your phone then?"

Felicity stopped jigging around and came over to him. "I can think of something we could do first while we're here on our own…" She moved closer, placed her arms around his shoulders and leant over until her lips met his…

And then they heard the key in the church door.

"Crap! It's my dad. Why the hell's he come back?" They instantly sprang apart; Felicity took Peter's hand again and dragged him back to their hiding place as the door opened.

Muttering how he was sure he had set the church alarm, the Professor strode back down the aisle as though he was about to disrupt a wedding. He marched up to the tomb of Sir Percival Fitzgerald and shone his flashlight slowly over it.

"Oh crap!" Felicity muttered in Peter's ear. "Oh crappity-crap."

As he put his light to one side, they watched in horror as he tried tentatively to lift the lid, first with one hand, then with two and then bucking his knees and really straining. They heard a faint noise. Stepping back satisfied, he picked up his phone again, turning the flashlight off. They saw him lift it to his ear and heard the faint dialling tone…

A strange and muffled version of Aretha Franklin's *Natural Woman* rent the air.

"Oh crappity-crappity-crap!" Felicity breathed softly, "he's dialling my number! I was right - my phone is in the tomb. I can't believe it still has some battery left!" Peter stifled a giggle and pressed his head into her shoulder so that he couldn't be heard. He felt Felicity shaking silently with laughter.

The man in front of them gave a yelp of surprise. He flung his own phone down and attacked the tomb lid with renewed energy. They saw him push the lid back, pick up his phone, switch on the flashlight and aim it into the tomb.

"Hey, hang on, who's that?" Felicity stopped laughing and whispered in his ear urgently. She crawled forward to see better. Peter joined her, peering round the base of the font.

A familiar figure was standing silently by the tomb watching the professor's antics. The professor, suddenly aware of someone, looked up. "Who's there," he asked curtly. "Maurice, is that you?" He shone his torch at the interloper.

"It's William!" Peter murmured to Felicity, hoping she would understand.

The watchers saw the professor stiffen as he took in the sight of William. Peter could not see William's face but suspected it would be quite something - an "I'm actually rather cross about you stealing my body" look, which would not be for the faint-hearted.

Felicity gasped as she realised that her father's flashlight was shining through the figure onto the wall behind. There was a sudden clatter and the light went out. Blackwell must have dropped his phone. He gave a desperate scream and started to back away from the phantom, crashing into the pew behind and falling over.

With a cry, Felicity scrambled to her feet and out of their hiding place. She dashed over to her fallen father.

"Dad, Dad, are you okay? It's me, Fliss!"

Peter realised that he was also going to have to reveal himself. Reluctantly he crawled out, ran over to the door and switched the main church lights on.

The watchman vanished. The man on the floor groaned and clutched his head. Peter could see bleeding.

"It's okay, Felicity, he's gone. Is your Dad all right?"

"I think he must have banged his head on the edge of the pew when he fell over."

Peter was about to retort that that would teach him not to steal skeletons, when he saw Felicity's face. Instead, he decided to be helpful. "I think I saw a first aid box in the vestry. I'll run and get it."

He dashed into the vestry and grabbed the box. When he returned, Blackwell was sitting up and Felicity was talking very tenderly to him.

"Now don't try to move Dad until we've checked out your head!" She had seated herself next to him on the cold tiles and was hugging him to her.

"But what are you doing here Fliss?" Professor Blackwell was utterly confused. "You should be at home. And your friend shouldn't come near us."

"And you shouldn't be trying to steal a skeleton," Felicity rebuked him sharply, removing her arms from his shoulders as she remembered why he had returned to the church.

"I…." He was lost for words, shuddering, clearly remembering the face of the skeleton's owner.

Peter took out some lint and a bandage and passed them over to Felicity. She carefully dressed her father's wound but her face was hardening. Clearly her sympathy for her wounded father was running out.

"Now He-who-steals-Skellies, we should really get you to A&E. Pete, could you fish my phone out of the tomb please. I'll see if there's enough battery power."

"I'm not sure you want to go to A&E at the moment because the hospitals are full of Covid patients." Peter leant deep into the tomb to fish out the phone. "I can't believe your battery's lasted this long!" He handed the phone over to her.

Just then there was a tremendous hammering on the church door.

"Open up! Whoever you are in there! OPEN UP!"

Blackwell groaned and put his hand to his injured head. Felicity and Peter looked at each other.

"Oh man, it's the Poliss!"

CHAPTER 41

"The Poliss" turned out, thankfully, to be Dad and the Rector - Dad having alerted her to the lights and noise coming from the church and the disappearance of Peter.

"Oh Professor Blackwell!" The Rector ran towards the figure on the floor and then skidded to a halt as she remembered the two-metre rule.

"Don't be too sympathetic," warned Felicity, "he's a thief!"

"Well, technically not. He didn't actually manage to steal anything," Peter pointed out.

"Well, a wannabe thief then!" Felicity glared at him. "Sorry Louise, but he was trying to nick the skeleton."

The Rector looked puzzled and looked round for it. "But why would he want to do that?"

"Because…" Felicity began.

"Because I'm an idiot." Blackwell pulled himself off the ground and sat on the pew facing them. He looked ashen-faced and the blood on his cheek was still glistening. "Because I'm a puffed-up idiot who thought it would be a good thing to obtain this" he gesticulated over to the tomb, "for my History Department as an object of curiosity. I didn't listen to my intelligent, and dare I say it, highly moralistic daughter when she told me it would be outright stealing. I have come to the rapid conclusion, after the events of tonight, that the skeleton in question should be given a proper burial in the churchyard with as much solemnity that the current rules permit." The Professor sank back into his seat, shattered.

The Rector now looked even more baffled. "You were going to steal Sir Percival Fitzgerald? Well, why didn't you say so -

you're welcome to him. He doesn't fit in here at all and his tomb blocking the north aisle technically puts us in breach of the Fire Regulations."

The professor looked exhausted and in pain, so Peter thought that he would explain.

"We've hidden the skeleton of William Wadsworth in the tomb of Sir Percival - come and have a look."

"But what are you doing here, our Peter? And who's this?" Now it was Dad's turn to look bewildered. He gesticulated towards Felicity with the look of someone completely out of their depth.

Peter wondered where even to begin, conscious of the fact that every reason for him being in the church was against the rules. Could he say he was simply taking photos in the churchyard when he heard Felicity calling for help?

"You tell them everything Peter." Felicity was still sitting on the floor. "It's all my fault that Pete broke the lockdown rules." She smiled at him and he felt brave again.

He turned to the Rector. "Felicity and I came into church the other night – she'd borrowed the key and we hid William's skeleton in Sir Percival's tomb as she knew her dad wanted to steal him. Then tonight we met again to try and find her phone which she'd accidentally left in church. We slipped in while Professor Blackwell was playing the organ and then he went away, and we were about to look for the phone and then he came back and we hid, and then…"

Peter broke off feeling that he was not the one to tell the next bit of the story. They found themselves plunged into an awkward silence. But help came from an unexpected direction.

Dad cleared his throat. "Reverend, er, Louise, you know we've been having trouble with Caleb seeing ghosts? Well, we've discovered, I mean, Pete has discovered, with us helping him, the whole story of William Wadsworth the Watchman. This is what we're going to tell you about tomorrow morning at the Zoom meeting - and, well if the Professor was trying to steal William's body then I can hazard a guess as to what might have happened just now..."

"I saw him!" The professor sat bolt upright once more. "I saw the ghost of a watchman standing over me. And I will take the look he gave me to my own grave!" He shuddered.

"Well yes, we've seen some of his more dramatic looks," Dad admitted. "But Peter and Caleb have shown us how he's a poor soul desperate to find peace. He was forced to lie under oath - a lie that caused an innocent lad to hang, and had to kill himself afterwards because he couldn't live with what he'd done."

"And we know that he *really* has to be buried in the churchyard," added Peter addressing the Rector directly.

The Rector realised that some decisive action was needed from her.

"It's very late and we are all breaking the law by even being in here. Tom and Peter, can I suggest we meet tomorrow morning on Zoom as planned. I've arranged for the rest of the church council to join us as the decision as to burials in the churchyard legally rests with them. I really want to hear the evidence - I do appreciate the work that you've been doing on this."

"Now Felicity." She turned to where Felicity sat with her father, still holding him tight. "Do you think you'll be able to get your father home? I suggest once you're there, you ring 111 to see what they say about treating head wounds and whether they think he needs to go to A&E. If he does need to go, then call me and we'll see what we can do."

"Now is everyone ready to leave right now?" There was no mistaking the tone in her voice. "Do we all have our phones? Everything else? Good. Now let's go!"

Felicity helped her father to his feet. Peter and Dad stood awkwardly by wanting to help but realising that they had to stay away. They shuffled slowly down the aisle and out into the churchyard, the Rector locking the door behind them. At the foot of the steps they stopped.

"Night Pete!" called Felicity. "It's been quite a day, hasn't it! Wouldn't have missed it for the world!" And she blew him a kiss.

"Night Fliss!" Peter 'caught' the kiss with his foot and pretended to kick it into an invisible goal, jubilantly cheering with his arms. She raised her eyes to the heavens and then started walking with her father towards the church gate.

Peter turned to follow his own father home. Out of habit they glanced up at the windows to see if William was lurking but there was no sign of him. Peter wondered if William's dramatic appearance at the tomb had exhausted his powers for the evening.

Mum, it transpired, had not exhausted her powers for the evening and was waiting in the kitchen to give him an earful. Caleb was sitting with her though it was way past his bedtime.

"Just what exactly do you think you're playing at staying out so late, breaking into the church in the dead of night - AGAIN I might add! Meeting up with strangers in complete contravention of all these new rules to stop Covid spreading. Do you think we're in this lockdown for the good of our health?"

"Well actually we are," Peter pointed out before he could stop himself.

Mum shot him a poisonous look. He sat down suddenly feeling very tired and mutinous. "Mum - I was…" But what was he doing? He was not quite sure he knew himself.

"He was helping a friend." Dad explained, sitting down at the table next to him, "two friends in fact."

"What? Professor Blackwell's not my friend!"

"No, but William is."

While he was pondering this new idea, his phone buzzed. It was Felicity.

"Dad's fine now. I dialled 111 and they said to make him rest and keep a watch to make sure he doesn't throw up or anything. So he's lying on the sofa and I'm keeping watch. Thanks for everything tonight. You were a star.

Mum's just called to give me the update on Kenneth. He's okay - they've taken him back to his sheltered housing and he's quite happy. The museum trustees are really pleased with us for breaking in and finding him LOL !!!!!

Oh and BTW Mum says you've got an epic story about William. She's going to put it out on Twitter and wants to interview you. You up for that?"

The idea terrified the very life out of him but he wasn't going to admit it. He quickly responded before he had time to change his mind.

"I will if you'll help me."

Meanwhile Dad had clearly been talking to Mum. When he stopped messaging, he found she was looking at him in a strange way. He raised his eyebrows at her. She suddenly laughed and came over to kiss him on the top of his head.

"Well, I'm right proud of you, our Peter! You've done a brilliant job with all this research. I'm forgetting that you're growing up fast." He looked down at the tablecloth, feeling his face burn scarlet.

Dad noticed the time. "Now come on gang, it's high time we were in bed. Don't forget we've got this meeting with the Rector and all those people on the church council tomorrow morning, and..." He broke off with a huge yawn.

"Can I do the talking?" Caleb, who had been gently nodding off, suddenly roused himself.

"We'll see," Dad replied, lifting him to his feet and propelling him towards the stairs.

CHAPTER 42

The meeting was supposed to start at eleven. At 10.59 am, Dad, Peter and Caleb were bunched together on the sofa, having propped up the iPad against a pile of hardback first edition Harry Potters, and had logged on. It was a hot morning, and at Caleb's insistence they were wearing shirts with ties to make a good impression. (Dad had his old tatty red shorts on but Peter and Caleb had promised to jump on him if he stood up while they were on Zoom.) Rascal was also there, lurking beneath the dining table, being scooped up from time to time and caressed by Caleb.

Only Mum was absent – she was banished to her pantry, sentenced to a morning of difficult meetings.

As they entered the meeting, the Rector, brightly lit and gleaming, gave them a welcoming wave but was busy trying to help the more elderly members of the council.

"Now June, you've got into the meeting but you're still not showing. Can you see the banner at the bottom of the screen? Yes? Well click on the picture of the microphone and on the video camera… oh well done!"

A rectangle of a lounge last decorated in the mid nineteen-eighties came into view, along with a face so ancient that at first they thought the screen had pixelated.

"Can you see me, Rector Louise?" the voice quavered.

The Rector gave her a thumbs up and then gave a long talk to everyone on how to indicate that they wanted to speak.

It was weird, Peter mused, to see all the church council lined up on the screen in front of him, as if each were a tiny rectangular flat in a large block. In the middle of the council members he spotted Felicity and Professor Blackwell – now sporting a large white bandage around his head. Felicity gave him a magnificent smile; Caleb responded by doing a crazy TikTok dance, blocking off the whole screen so that they nearly missed their cue from the Rector. She was still speaking in the same dull tone, but in the nick of time they realised she was describing the finding of the skeleton. Physically forcing Caleb to sit back down, Peter and Dad started to listen more attentively.

The Rector concluded her introduction by saying that she now had the certificate from the police to say they were not treating the discovery as suspicious, so if the council decided that the skeleton should not be given a churchyard burial, he could go back into its old grave.

"NO!" Caleb shouted to the screen. A second later the screen wobbled as fifteen people flinched.

Dad put a calming arm round him. "Ssshh - remember what we decided. I'm to go first." So Dad started to talk - explaining how the grave of William Wadsworth had been discovered in the building site next to the church and that during lockdown they had started a project to see what they could find out about it.

And then it was Peter's turn. Staring at the little screen, he recounted that, after reading Professor Blackwell's book, they had learned about the rise of Joseph Merceron and the execution of Nathaniel Daykin for killing a watchman – condemned on the evidence of another watchman, William Wadsworth, who had witnessed Daykin enter the churchyard through the wicket gate.

It was hard work talking over Zoom. Although he could see everyone's face, there was little to read on any of them. His own face however, clearly visible in the right-hand corner of the screen, was extremely off-putting. Catching a glimpse of his serious furrowed brow, he lost concentration and then faltered. The on-screen Peter stopped too and now bore a rabbit-caught-in-headlights look. Sensing he was losing his audience, the first swells of panic started to wash over him.

Crap, he couldn't bottle it now! Not with so much at stake?

CHAPTER 43

Razzy-Razzy-Rascal, I don't know WHAT is happening to Peter because he's just stopped dead and has this completely DUMB look on his face as though he's TOTALLY AND UTTERLY lost the plot - or perhaps he's has actually managed (after MANY years of trying) to BORE himself to death?

And I can see some of the old people have got frozen expressions on their face and either they've got rubbish Wi-Fi or they've ACTUALLY DOZED OFF.

And the Rector's got this 'what the heck is happening, why did I let these kids into my precious meeting' look about her. So I lean forward and speaking at them REALLY REALLY LOUDLY and this works because I can see that everyone's waking up and starting to PAY ATTENTION!!!

So I tell them the bit about us knowing that William was the watchman because we found his name in the church records AS FAST AS I CAN because it's really dull. And then I can get to the REALLY EXCITING BIT - about not being able to see the wicket gate from our window therefore PROVING THAT WILLIAM LIED!!!!

But then Dad gets cross with me because he says that we agreed Peter could tell them about that bit and so Pete takes over again (he's now lost his glazed sheep look) and tells them about us finding where the wicket gate was - and that's *why* he could tell that William had lied at the trial. And, despite the fact I had to rescue him from his NEAR DEATH experience, he still gives me one of his STUPID SMUG LOOKS so I thump him and so Dad has to get up to take me out and so EVERYONE GETS TO SEE HIS SHORTS!

And I can't hear anything through the door, even though I try that trick where you hold a glass up to it and stick your ears to the glass, (and it's A LOAD OF RUBBISH so don't bother even trying it or perhaps we've got too thick doors?) but FINALLY Dad comes out and tells me I can go back in IF I AM GOOD.

And Peter and Dad have finished and the church people are talking to each other and the Rector is finding it difficult cos some of them are talking and we can't hear them and they've forgotten they're stuck ON MUTE. And Peter and Dad are looking nervous. And I can see Felicity and I give her a wave and she waves back but she looks scared too.

And then that REALLY REALLY OLD LADY who we can hardly make out cos she has TOO MANY WRINKLES raises her hand and I think she wants to go to THE LOO. But she doesn't - she wants to speak. And she says in this high shaky voice "but the fact remains, Reverend Louise, the man did kill himself and that is an UNFORGIVABLE SIN against nature".

And Dad and Pete and Me and Felicity and Professor Blackwood (still with his BANDAGE on his head) all put our hands up. But the Rector thinks she's got this one covered and gives the OLD BAT a rather pointless lecture on what we know about mental health having changed over time and it was now permitted to bury people who had killed themselves in churchyards…snore…snore…snore.

I am holding my hand up SO HIGH NOW THAT I'M STANDING UP and so finally the Rector sees me and says I can speak.

And I tell them that William was SCARED STIFF of Merceron – probably because Merceron had killed Samuel Weaver his boss. And he couldn't help it and that was why he KILLED HIMSELF because he was COMPLETELY AND TOTALLY sorry about what he had done.

And the Rector thanks me and says that she now needs EVERYONE on the Council (that's everyone over a hundred except for her and Felicity's dad) to say whether they are for or against William being buried in the churchyard. And I can tell the Rector's really on our side because she calls him by his name rather than 'the skeleton'. And everyone's saying yes and well done boys and what a good job and all that until she comes to the REALLY REALLY OLD LADY who says that she's sorry but she's AGAINST THE MOTION.

And that's it.

William has to be reburied in his old grave and WE'VE LOST.

And I crawl back under the dining table and stay there as there's

NO POINT in coming out.

CHAPTER 44

After the decision of the meeting they were expecting some sort of backlash from the watchman. But despite Caleb's pre-emptive hiding under the table, there was nothing. It was as though he, like them, had simply given up and could not even be bothered to flicker the candle flame.

Felicity and Professor Blackwell had come round to their doorstep to offer their commiserations - the professor looking a hundred times better than he had the previous evening. The Rector had phoned to say how sorry she was and that she could try to talk to the dissenting council member.

"But don't get your hopes up. She's a very," here the Rector had paused looking for the right word, "a very principled lady."

Peter lay back on his bed thoroughly dejected. The Rector had been kind and sympathetic but he'd just wanted to punch her, and had had to run outside into the churchyard to kick stones and gravel until the anger left him. Now he just wanted to lie on his bed and stare at the ceiling.

Caleb had refused to come out from under the dining table and had made a series of protest signs which he'd stuck to the legs of the dining chairs.

> **THIS IS AN OFFICIAL SIT IN FOR EVERY DAY WILLIAM WADSWORTH IS NOT BURIED IN THE CHURCHYARD**
> **PUT FOOD HERE →**
> **PUT DRINK HERE ↓**
> **NOW BOG OFF!!**

"We are doubly upset," Mum told Peter at teatime when she had emerged from her pantry and come upstairs to find him. "Not only do we feel like all our hard work has been for nothing, it's like we're in mourning for William because we've got to know his sad story. But Pete, we have to remember that all around us there are people who have lost people to Covid and aren't even able to have a proper funeral for them. On the BBC just now, there was a terrible story about a thirteen-year-old lad from Bethnal Green who's died of Covid all alone in hospital. Now how awful is that! Think about him and his family, will you – and try and get a bit of perspective on this."

Peter glared at her, his misery now compounded by guilt. Mum softened.

"Come on down for your tea, love. Being hungry won't make you feel any better. And you can bear witness to the moment when Cay realises he needs the loo and can't get out."

Just then there was a tremendous ratatat-tating at the front door. They looked at each other in surprise. A voice called up from the street.

"Pete, Pete open up. I've got some news!"

"It's Fliss!" Peter tore downstairs casting his misery off like a winter coat. Dad was already unlocking the door and the sounds of furniture violently being shifted indicated that Caleb was trying to get out of his barricade.

It was indeed Felicity. She was bubbling over with excitement and waving her phone at Peter.

"It's Mum! She says her post on Twitter about your watchman has gone viral. People have been reading the story all over the world – all about you figuring out that William couldn't have seen Nathaniel in the churchyard, about us breaking into the museum to get that letter – and being caught by a real watchman! And she wants to talk to you." With this, she tapped the speaker button and her mother's voice filled the street.

"So, Peter the Great, we meet in more auspicious circumstances. Or rather I hope so - I'm assuming you're not currently in the process of burglarizing any more heritage premises?"

"No Professor Moore," Peter grinned, feeling Dad's curiosity burning into his back.

"Call me Angela, please." But it seemed the voice had little time for niceties. "I have some news for you, Peter. Your research has attracted much interest and not just in academic circles. My tweets have been retweeted thousands of times already and I've had some wonderful responses - all very sympathetic to William and all saying that he must be buried in the churchyard. What do you think?"

"That's cool, really cool." (What the heck was he supposed to say?)

The voice continued. "Now, do you think if we showed the Reverend Lousie how many folk are interested in this matter, she'd change her mind?"

Peter sighed. "I don't think she would," he explained politely. "You see, the decision on burials in the churchyard has to taken by the church council and if one person objects, then that's it."

"And that's it? You're going to let one person spoil this whole thing?" The voice on the other end of the phone sounded incredulous.

"But the old lady's very, very old and, well I'm not sure how you fight against a very old person."

"There's always a way, Peter, always a way." The voice sounded reassuring. "And you don't need to be aggressive or anything like that. You just have a good think, and I will make sure my little media storm comes to the attention of the right people. Well Peter, it's been a pleasure to talk to you again and I hope we get to meet properly soon."

"Erm.. thanks Professor Mummy – oh, crap sorry, I mean Professor Moore!" His stomach gave a lurch as he felt a proper idiot.

The voice gave a great boom of laughter, warm and friendly. "Don't worry Peter. I know my dear daughter well! Now would you pass me back?"

Felicity took the phone. She gave him a merry smile as she set off home, still talking to her mum. He turned round to see his own family hanging around the front door.

"You heard that?"

"Yes. Good of her to write about it." Dad commented hopefully. "Surely the Rector can't re-inter the body now?"

"I don't know," said Mum pessimistically. "If the church council decisions have to be unanimous, then they have to be unanimous. The only thing that will change the Rector's mind, is if the really really old lady changes hers – oh come on, she must have a name?"

"She's called June," announced Caleb begrudgingly as if even her name said out loud cast a further shadow of gloom onto the evening.

"Well let's have tea," Dad ushered them into the kitchen, "and maybe we can think of a way to persuade June, as we know a thousand twittering Americans won't."

"Several thousand and not necessarily American," Mum was ever pedantic. "Now I wouldn't usually have my phone out at the dinner table, but I am going to check her feed to see what's actually being said."

They ate their meal in silence as Mum showed them Professor Moore's ever-evolving Twitter feed.

"This is very weird!" Dad announced after a bit.

"I know!" Peter laughed. "There's a "#whatisablunderbuss" thread going round!"

"Well, what is a blunderbuss?" Caleb asked, playing with his spaghetti.

"It's a type of old-fashioned shotgun." Peter told him. There was a thought nagging him - something he needed to remember.

Mum was googling the term. "Hmm, 'blunderbuss, from the Dutch 'donderbus' meaning thunder pipe'. Known as dragons because of the noise and smoke they made - hence the name 'dragoons' given to the soldiers that used them. Not sure it would be the easiest thing to kill yourself with, but I suppose you could saw the end off, or even pull the trigger with a string…" She stopped, seeing Caleb's face. "Sorry Cay," she leaned over and hugged him. "I'm getting carried away a bit aren't I."

"Let's have some pudding," Dad had made their favourite sticky toffee pudding in his attempt to cheer them up. There was another knock at the door. Mum pulled a face at the disruption and went to answer it.

"I thought we were supposed to be all in lockdown," Dad growled. Caleb giggled and then stopped short as they could hear raised voices.

"No – best stay put," Dad told them as they made to get up. "Your mum's quite capable of handling it on her own." They heard the sound of the front door shutting and Mum came back in, her face flushed. She sat back down at the table and took a gulp of water.

"Well I give you Exhibit A - a well and truly annoyed clergywoman!"

"The Rector's seen Twitter?" Peter guessed.

"Yes - and she's perfectly and understandably furious that her church's name is being bandied around the world without her permission - hence her long lecture to me about the fact that we should have gone to her first before putting it out there."

"But we didn't!" Peter protested, though realising that he had agreed to it.

"Oh don't worry – her other issue is that the tweets mention your poor watchman, Kenneth. Even though he's not actually named, she seems to think that's a breach of his privacy. I told her that technically it wasn't and, well, that didn't help.

Oh, I don't think we've done anything wrong," Mum attempted to reassure Peter. "She's just thoroughly annoyed that all these people are telling her to let William be buried in the churchyard - something that legally she can't do."

"So how did you leave it?" Dad asked.

Mum was about to start to eat her pudding but put her spoon down again. "I said that we hadn't meant to insult Kenneth at all, and that we respected the time the church council had given to us this morning to tell our story. And that if we came across any further evidence to change June's mind, we would bring it to her attention first. She said that we'd better be quick about it because the archaeologist is coming over tomorrow morning to put the skeleton back in his old grave."

"Tomorrow morning!" Caleb shrieked. "We must hide him again!"

"Please," Mum said, fighting her impatience. "Let me finish my pudding first!"

CHAPTER 45

For her own reasons, the Rector had not asked them to help the archaeologist rebury the skeleton and for the most part Peter did not care. He woke in the morning with a feeling of foreboding, as if he was waiting to sit a really hard exam.

The weather did not help. The sun shone amiably underneath a sapphire sky and the few clouds that there were moved gently and happily along.

Caleb (after a decent breakfast) had gone straight into his den, officially back on strike. Peter knew he had the iPad with him because he could hear the muffled sounds of his favourite computer game. Mum was back in her pantry. Dad had started to put some more shelves up - this time in the front bedroom. Peter privately suspected Dad was developing an addiction to putting shelves up and soon every wall in the Watch House would be covered in shelving so the place would be like living in a cramped version of Sainsburys.

At least he had his phone to talk to Felicity. But even that did not give him any pleasure this morning. Felicity's first message: "my mum's contacted the Rector and she still says no," made him worry about what they might do next. Much as he resented June for her stance, he still felt bad about her being condemned by a million tweets. And after Professor Moore's challenge to him to not give up, he also felt like a proper failure.

He rose and wandered listlessly over to the window. A movement caught his eye and he watched as a car pulled up at the building site, recognising the short figure who got out. It was the archaeologist - clearly there to start work preparing the old grave to receive back its body. He turned away, remembering the day he and Mum had carried the body to the church. He recalled the rusty red colour of the bones and how smooth the skull was, seemingly with minimal damage from its time in the earth.

Something that had been echoing around his subconscious started to nag him again and he turned away to head downstairs for a drink. As he reached the bottom of the stairs, he could hear the sounds of Caleb's game – the one where you played as a heavily-armed mercenary, fighting off zombie pirates. Despite his brother's sensitivities over ghosts, blood, animals being hurt (the list was long and increasingly so) Caleb still enjoyed games such as these where the graphics were incredibly gruesome. Dad had once had to retire from playing quite green in the face after blasting a pirate chief's head off.

And then he realised!

The blunderbuss! William had killed himself with his own blunderbuss – Martha's letter had said so. Now, leaving aside the fact that it was rather tricky to pull a shotgun trigger when it was aimed on yourself, surely blasting yourself at close range would leave a mark?

With a shout to Dad to follow him, Peter dashed outside and raced across the churchyard to find the archaeologist. She was now inside the church and was rather startled to find Peter bearing down on her.

"The skeleton!" he gasped, "the skeleton - can I have another look at him please?"

By the time Dad caught up with them, Peter and the archaeologist, carefully trying to keep two metres apart from each other, had lifted the skeleton out of the tomb and were laying him gently on the tiled floor. Peter stepped back. The archaeologist immediately got to work with her torch and scalpel. After making a careful examination, she picked up the skull carefully and held it towards them.

"Well I am not a forensic scientist, but I can safely say that this skeleton has no marks on his body that would suggest he was killed by a blunderbuss. In fact, he's remarkably intact except for this interesting mark on the back of his skull."

Dad and Peter craned their necks to see. There was a faint copper dent about two inches long.

"Do you think that could be a head wound?"

"I would have to ask an expert, but I wouldn't be surprised. Now, I have seen something like this before when I was working on an excavation of a medieval battle site near Shrewsbury. We came across several skulls with this sort of injury - our pathology expert said that they were likely caused by a blunt weapon such as a club. The soldier would be knocked out cold from behind by the enemy and then could be finished off by a knife to the heart." She stopped short as the Rector came into the church.

"Good morning," the Rector began cheerily and then saw Dad and Peter.

"He didn't commit suicide," Peter told her bluntly. "He was supposed to have killed himself with his own blunderbuss. That's what Mrs de la Court's letter said. "But look – his skull is still intact. There's absolutely no way he killed himself with his own blunderbuss!"

"And if you look here," Dad pointed to the back of the skull still in the archaeologist's hand, "you can see the mark of the weapon that hints at how he was actually killed." He looked up at the archaeologist who quickly repeated her battle site story.

The Rector immediately realised the significance of what he said. "So you mean he was…"

"Murdered!" Peter announced boldly. "Knocked out and then stabbed. Probably by Merceron or one of his men. I mean there's no way we can prove it - but it all seems to point to that. Especially after what Nathaniel's mum reckoned happened to Samuel Weaver."

They stared at the skull who stared back at them through its eyeless sockets with its eternal grin.

"So let me get this straight, our Peter." Dad was ensuring he had the facts right. "Joseph Merceron killed Samuel Weaver …"

"Because Weaver objects to the body-snatching scam?" Peter suggested.

"Quite possibly - though there's no evidence. But then Merceron deliberately frames Nat Daykin for the murder using our William…" Dad was quickly adding things up.

"Whom he tries to pay off, but it doesn't work and Merceron then has to kill William to keep him quiet…" Now the Rector was putting her mind to the problem.

"And Merceron puts it around that William killed himself!" Peter ended in triumph and then realised that this might not be something you celebrated so rapturously.

He turned to the Rector.

"Will it stand up in court – I mean, will this convince June that William didn't kill himself?"

"Excuse me, did I hear my name mentioned?"

A very precise elderly voice interrupted their discussion. They spun round to see the ancient old lady leaning against a richly decorated walking stick at the church entrance.

The Rector, looking puzzled and vaguely alarmed, walked towards her parishioner, stopping at a distance away and raising her voice. "June, lovely to see you, but you mustn't come in here because you could catch Covid. I know we shouldn't be in here either, but it is a bit of an emergency. Peter…"

"But it's Peter I need to speak to. If I wait in the churchyard, will the young man come out to speak to me please?" The old lady shrank back and disappeared from view.

Dad and Peter looked at each other bewildered. Peter shrugged. "I guess I'd better go and see what she wants." He rose to his feet and walked out of the church.

June was sitting on a bench in the sunshine, her eyes closed and arms held together out in front of her as though she was praying. Feeling nervous, Peter stopped two metres away from her and coughed gently.

"Are you Peter?" the old lady opened her eyes. "You're more handsome in real life than on that silly screen." Peter found himself blushing and offered his own private prayer of thanks that Caleb was not hearing this.

But the old lady continued in her quaint voice. "I find myself in your debt Peter. It transpires that you and Miss Blackwell have done a rather important thing for me."

"I'm sorry?" He was truly baffled.

"My daughter phoned me last night from the States where she lives. She had read Angela Moore's blog about the security guard being discovered living in the museum, and wanted to know whether it was Kenneth - her brother."

Realisation hit Peter like a gust of wind on a hot day. "You're Kenneth's mum?"

The old lady looked up at him and her form seemed to diminish even more in front of his eyes. "Yes, young man, but not a very good one I'm afraid to say." Her voice tailed off and a tear started to trickle down her brittle cheeks. "My son Kenneth has special needs and lives in sheltered housing in Hackney. Ever since we went into lockdown, I've been trying to get hold of him but he never has his phone switched on. As I couldn't get to see him, I just trusted he was safely at his home." June's voice now rose in anguish. "I thought his carers would have told me that he was missing - I'd no idea he'd become imprisoned in that museum. It breaks my heart to think that he was so neglected…" She broke off, her voice breaking into silent sobs, her shoulders shaking.

Peter felt that he had moved beyond being embarrassed. A cloud passed in front of the sun and a strange numbness crept over him. After what seemed like hours, to his utter relief, June stopped crying and looked intently at him.

"It was you wonderful children who discovered him." This came out like an accusation.

"Erm…well yes it was…"

"So Peter, what can I do to say thank you?"

CHAPTER 46

June was looking directly up at him, her baby blue eyes hopeful with anticipation. The sun came out again and the trees of the churchyard were illuminated in vivid colour once more. Peter stared at her, not knowing what to say. Then the idea sounded in his head like a car horn. It was so obvious he gasped.

"Mrs... er ... June, there is one thing you could do for us." He could see hope dawning in her eyes. "Please could you give permission for William to be buried in the churchyard? You might have heard us just now - we've discovered that he didn't kill himself cos he was murdered."

Quickly Peter filled her in. The old lady sat silent for a moment and then looked up at him. "My dear boy, of course he can be buried in the churchyard" She sighed and wiped away her remaining tears. "I can see that I was wrong – quite wrong. And it appears that the poor soul does after all deserve a peaceful resting place. Yes, I gratefully give permission and I will go and tell Rector Louise this minute. It is the least I can do."

Peter watched as, using her stick with precision, she got to her feet. The Rector, the archaeologist and Dad had come out of the church and were standing, sensibly spaced out, by the entrance, their faces a picture of puzzlement. As June recounted her decision to the Rector, Peter saw Dad's wondering face and gave him the thumbs up.

The Rector smiled at them all. "Now June's made her decision I propose I call an emergency council meeting for this evening. Excuse me - I'd better go and start phoning round." And she marched off down the church path.

The archaeologist, who had been trying to keep up with the conversation and failing, interrupted their thoughts. "Do I take it that the skeleton needs to stay here for the time being? Because if so, I'll put it back into the casket."

Dad was looking with dismay at the plastic box the archaeologist was holding in her hands. "If he's going to get a proper burial, he'll need something better than this. I've an idea." He set off quickly back to the Watch House, clearly a man on a mission.

"You'd better scoot too," the archaeologist told Peter. "Remember we're supposed to be in lockdown."

"Oh right. Thanks very much anyway for your help."

"You're welcome. I don't get many days like this, I can tell you." She gave him a cheerful look and then turned to go back inside. As she started up the church steps, something dropped from the plastic casket.

"Hang on, you've dropped your paper!" Peter ran forward and picked it up from the stone pavement. The archaeologist turned and held out a spare hand.

"Cheers - it's my job sheet. I still need that. Hey what's the matter?"

Peter was staring at the page as though he had seen a ghost. "*De la Court Holdings.*"

The archaeologist frowned. "The developers who hired me to carry out the excavation? It's a huge property company - one of London's biggest."

"Do they own the land where the skeleton was found?"

"Of course. I think they own most of the land around here except for the glebe land – the church land, that is."

Peter's mind was racing so fast that his words stumbled out of his mouth. "Is it possible that they owned the land way back when William was buried there?"

The archaeologist nodded. "Yes, entirely possible. De la Court Holdings has been around for a very long time. It's why they've got such a huge presence in London."

"Oh man! That's sweet. Absolutely sweet!" Leaving the archaeologist wondering, Peter practically skipped out of church. He sat down on the bench and face-timed Felicity. She answered instantly, her green eyes looking quizzically at him.

"Oh Fliss I've got so much to tell you!" Where to start? He quickly related the events of the morning - his realisation about William's injuries, June's confession and her relenting over William's burial. Felicity's eyes grew wider as he started to tell her about De la Court Holdings.

"So that merchant, Francis de la Court - Martha''s second husband, must have buried William on land he owned - as close to consecrated land as physically possible. They must have figured he was as much a victim of Merceron as Nathaniel had been and probably guessed that Merceron had had him murdered. And I reckon that's why they gave him a headstone and a decent coffin!"

He finished and Felicity clapped her hands like a happy seal.

"That's absolutely amazing, Peter-the-so-swaggeringly-Great – you are a flippin' genius! Everything fits perfectly! And I cannot *believe* June is Kenneth's mum! That is, like, one incredible coincidence. But I'm so glad we were able to help him."

"Perhaps it was destiny or something? I mean, we investigate why a ghostly watchman is bugging us, and then end up rescuing a real watchman!"

"That's rather too spooky!" Felicity laughed slightly uneasily and changed the subject. "So what's happening next - spill the tea."

"They're having an emergency meeting tonight so that they can take another vote on whether William can be buried in the churchyard."

"I can't wait to tell Mum and all her followers! Do you mind if I do? They'll be on their knees waiting for the verdict!"

Peter felt a slight qualm. "Erm, perhaps it's best not to tell them too much about June being Kenneth's mum. Better to tell them all about us finding out that he was murdered by Merceron and it's that that's changed the council's mind. I mean, that's got to be more interesting hasn't it." Then he laughed. "This is so crazy. All these people in the world waiting for the decision of a church council to let an ancient skeleton be buried in a churchyard!"

"We create the news, Pete – that's what people say anyway. Most of the time I reckon it's a load of crap but this time…"

"Wish I could see you again, on our own I mean." This was out before he could stop himself.

"Me too, Peter. You're one amazing guy! Let's make a plan!"

Peter's grin grew even wider. He sat there in the sunshine in locked-down London, the air pumping out bird song and the plane trees dancing. He had captured the truth and brought it home.

CHAPTER 47

So Razzy-Razzy-Rascal, you won't believe this (but cats never believe anything anyway cos they're just cats so it doesn't really matter) but we've just had another of those Zoom meetings with the old people from the church and the really really old lady has agreed that WILLIAM CAN BE BURIED IN THE CHURCHYARD!!!!!

It's cos Felicity and Peter did that mad thing and broke into that museum place and Felicity was kidnapped by this lonely security guard who turned out to be the really really old lady's son - which is a such a FREAKY coincidence that the Rector said that GOD MUST have had a hand in it. And my spine went ALL TINGLY when she said it but perhaps there is something ACTUALLY in it?

And Felicity got her mum to post the verdict on Twitter and they were all jumping around getting STUPIDLY DAFT, as my mum says, watching the tweets being retweeted and all that. And Felicity and Pete are NOW standing in the churchyard doing this dance thing that they're putting out on TikTok which is INCREDIBLY EMBARRASSING. (But I don't really mind because I know William's HAPPY and that's all that matters really).

And the Rector's dropping off some forms for Mum and Dad to fill in so that the funeral can take place tomorrow. She says she is going to treat us as WILLIAM'S FAMILY as we've been behaving as such, but then she said she WOULDN'T CHARGE US for the funeral. (Dad asked cos he worries about stuff like that).

And Professor Blackwell, who's COMPLETELY on our side now and everything since William SCARED THE SMELLY BROWN PANTS OFF HIM !!!, says he will play the cello at the grave side (we have got to have the funeral outside as the church is supposed to be ABSOLUTELY OUT OF BOUNDS EVEN FOR RECTORS) and Felicity will play the violin. And Felicity looked a BIT SURPRISED by this but then nodded and said yes she would as it was for William.

And Dad's making a COFFIN in our back yard using some of the wood he was using for the new shelves. He says I can help him plane the wood once he's sawn it all into the right shape. Planing is where you scrape off the top layer of the wood, leaving the smooth bit underneath which you then vanish. Mum says I mustn't drop the plane on my foot cos we can't go to A&E because the hospital's too busy with Covid.

And Mum has washed all our shirts so that we can look REALLY SMART tomorrow and she's even going to iron them which is MAJOR NEWS because Mum so HATES ironing. And she's found a black tie for Dad to wear so it's all official.

So I'm looking forward to it - which is a bit strange as I don't know whether you're allowed to look forward to funerals?

And I've got to go because the man from the council has just brought round one of those tiny 1CX JCBs to dig the actual grave and the Rector says I can watch if I STAY WELL BACK.

And Dad says no, I can't have a go….

CHAPTER 48

And so, two hundred and twenty-five years late, William Wadsworth, former watchman of the parish, was laid to rest in St Wilfred's churchyard beneath the rustling plane trees.

Peter, with his long lockdown hair brushed as neatly as possible, and Dad suited and freshly shaven, acted as pallbearers. Carrying the neat coffin on their shoulders, they walked at a steady sombre pace from the church door to the newly-dug grave. The Rector was waiting for them, standing at the other side of the grave, robes on and her prayer book open.

Away to their left, Professor Blackwell and Felicity were playing something beautiful and Baroque. Peter almost dropped his end of the coffin when he clapped eyes on Felicity. Her shimmering mass of curly hair was magnificent in the sunlight and she was wearing a deep blue dress that swayed as her arm swung to and fro.

Mum and Caleb stood well away from the grave. The Rector had been insistent that legally only five people could be in attendance which including herself and the musicians, but there was nothing to stop them watching from the back door of the Watch House. Indeed, Peter saw with a shock that brought a sudden lump to his throat, that outside the churchyard, arranged at safe intervals behind the black railings, were the church council members - each dressed in black and looking profoundly solemn. June was there among them, dressed in something that looked like it dated from William's era, if not earlier. And from the building site, the archaeologist peered over the wall watching.

The music came to an end. The Rector took a deep breath and began, her strident tones sounding above the birdsong.

"I KNOW that my Redeemer liveth, and that he shall stand at the latter day upon the earth. And though after my skin worms destroy this body, yet in my flesh shall I see God: whom I shall see for myself, and mine eyes shall behold, and not another."

Back beneath the trees Mum gave a gasp of annoyance as her phone buzzed. She reached inside her handbag to switch it off, whispered to Caleb and then disappeared into the house. Caleb stayed where he was, watching as the Rector continued with the burial service.

Peter and Dad at the graveside managed well with the ropes to lower the coffin into the grave – the practice session the previous evening paying dividends. The ropes retrieved, the coffin sat snugly in the earth, ready for Felicity to throw the first clod onto the lid.

Then the Rector led them in the Lord's Prayer, Dad pronouncing the words boldly as his memories of Sunday school resurfaced; Peter whispering it, glad that he had had to memorise it at school for RE so that he didn't look like an idiot.

Caleb listened as the prayer was taken up by the watchers outside the churchyard so that the atmosphere was full of the ancient words and for a brief moment it felt like the very stones of the church were praying too.

"For thine is the Kingdom, the Power and the Glory, forever and ever. Amen."

The Amen echoed around, fading over time as the last person sent up their prayer.

Then, as if the wind started to blow once more onto the sails of a becalmed ship, people started to move away. Felicity and her father started to play again. The Rector closed her book and, nodding to Peter and Dad, moved off briskly back to the Rectory to disrobe. Caleb felt Mum reappear by his side. She gently took his hand in hers.

"Sorry about that, love. It was a call from one of our major clients - but I did run upstairs to watch from your bedroom. And guess what?"

Peter and Dad strolled over to join them, Peter noting Mum's face was glowing with excitement.

"Guess what - I saw him! William!"

"In the house?" Peter asked puzzled and slightly perturbed.

"No - in the churchyard! He was standing between the house and the grave – with his back to me but dressed in his uniform as you've told me, with his hat and his rattle hanging by his side. As you all were saying The Lord's Prayer this amazing thing happened. He turned and looked up at me – as though he knew I was watching. And I saw his face and, guess what? He gave me the most beautiful smile. Then he saluted and turned away and started to walk towards the grave. And at that moment the sun came out and shone right down between the trees and he seemed to vanish into it so that I couldn't see him anymore."

Peter looked at his mother and saw that tears were pouring down her face. Caleb was crying too. He put his arm round them and held them close.

"Oh, come on! You'll set me off with all your roaring!" Dad pulled out a tissue and blew his own nose loudly.

Peter was saved by a shout from behind him. He wheeled round. Felicity and Professor Blackwell had packed up and were about to leave.

"See you soon Peter the Great!" Felicity blew him a kiss - which took a moment to do as she was carrying both her violin case and music stand.

"Bravo chaps! That was a jolly good thing we did today." The professor waved at them and then instruments in hand they left the churchyard.

Peter turned back to his family. Dad had his arms around Mum and Caleb as they wiped their eyes. A thought struck him.

"So you finally did get to see him, Mum."

His mother smiled. "Yes and I reckon I'm the very last person to ever see him."

"Were you charging the client all this time you were gawping at a ghost?" Dad chided gently.

"Oh, shut up, Tom!" Mum laughed and punched her husband's arm.

"Time for elevenses?" Caleb asked hopefully.

THE REAL WATCH HOUSE

The Watch House in this story is based on the Watch House of St Matthew's Church in Bethnal Green, London. The Reverend Joshua King and the church warden of St Matthew's, Joseph Merceron, were real people - the latter nearly as big a villain as this story makes out. The plot, however, involving William and Nathaniel and all the other characters in this story, is completely made up.

The real Watch House can be found on the corner of St Matthews Row and Wood Close: it's a striking square block of a building with the name "The Watch House" over the front entrance, so you can't really miss it. As Peter and Caleb find out, it was indeed built in 1754 to house watchmen to guard against the body-snatchers who provided corpses for dissection to the local hospitals.

The eighteenth century is sometimes referred to as 'the Age of Enlightenment' because people started to question the world as they knew it and many scientific and medical discoveries were made. It did however have its downside – the surgeons at the schools of medicine at the new London hospitals were content not to ask too many questions as to where the bodies for their research and teaching actually came from - hence the lucrative business of body-snatching.

Provided with a blunderbuss and the permission to fire it (but only after sounding a rattle) the watchmen living at the Watch House were paid a reward of 2 guineas for the apprehension of any body snatchers. (This right is still held by the churchwardens of St Matthews today!)

In 1809 Joshua King became Rector of St Matthews and took a close personal interest in the goings-on at the parish in Bethnal Green. (This was unusual - most rectors at that time would instead pay a poor curate to live and work in the parish while they themselves would live in comparative luxury somewhere much more pleasant.) King uncovered a dreadful trail of corruption led by the churchwarden Joseph Merceron. This unsavoury character ran all sorts of criminal practices. King struggled for some years to bring him to justice and finally managed to send him to prison in 1818.

The Reverend King left the parish shortly after this and never returned. On his release from prison, Merceron, finding his nemesis gone, promptly restarted up all his old 'businesses' and carried on his criminal activities until his death in 1861. You can see Merceron's tomb in the church – only one of two to survive bomb attacks on the church in the Blitz. It states he 'lived to an honourable old age!"

THE LOCKDOWN OF 2020

In the first months of 2020 the coronavirus pandemic, Covid-19, arrived in the United Kingdom, having already caused immense suffering in other parts of the world. In mid-March the country went into lockdown. People were told to stay at home and not go out except to buy food and for exercise. Churches were locked up and services started to be held online. Schools were closed and children had to do work provided for them by their schools online. Museums and galleries were closed up and those unable to work were put on furlough - the Government would pay most of their wages while they were unable to work. Funerals could be held (and sadly there were many) but had to be held outside with only five people in attendance. Food shops and the supermarkets were allowed to remain open but had to have restricted entry, so people would queue up outside, standing two metres apart.

During this time, Clap for our Carers happened every Thursday at 8pm. People would come out onto their doorsteps, driveways and balconies to clap, bang pans, ring bells and make some noise to say thank you to the NHS and for all others who were working to keep things going during the pandemic. They also took the opportunity to have a good catch up with neighbours. Once people got over the embarrassment, it was actually good fun - and yes, they did clap for carers in Yorkshire despite Caleb's doubts.

AND ONE FINAL THING...

Felicity states that her mother, Professor Angela Moore, is only one of only twenty-six black female professors in the UK. In 2018, a report commissioned by the University and College Union showed that there were just twenty-five Black British female professors in UK universities, the smallest group of professors in terms of both race and gender. So, as Felicity would say, all a bit crap.

ABOUT THE AUTHOR

Bridget R. Edwards

Bridget has been writing since childhood - her first work was an adaption of "A Christmas Carol" which she, her brother and their friends performed in the garage. Bridget wrote this book for her godsons who were living in the real Watch House in Bethnal Green at the time. Originally from Yorkshire, Bridget now lives in Hertfordshire with her husband, daughters and a handsome labradoodle. Aside from writing, Bridget loves hiking and playing the flute (she would love to play the euphonium, but that's next year's project).

BOOKS BY THIS AUTHOR

Who Minds The Minder

COMING SOON

It's summer 2020. Back up north and buoyed by their success with the Watchman, Caleb advertises their services as ghosthunters. Peter, Caleb and Felicity are hired to investigate the appearance of the ghost of a dinner lady at their old school. But things turn nasty when Peter's old nemesis, Jake Webb, learns that Peter is back in town. Before long it becomes clear that the school, and Peter himself, are in deadly danger!

UNTITLED

Printed in Great Britain
by Amazon